CW01095601

DEATH IN THE CLOSET

AN EDWARD CRISP MYSTERY

PETER BOON

Copyright © June 2021 Peter Boon

Published by Meadowcroft Publishing

This is a work of fiction. Names, characters, businesses, places, events, locales, and incidents are either the products of the author's imagination or used in a fictitious manner. Any resemblance to actual persons, living or dead, or actual events is purely coincidental.

All rights reserved. No part of this book may be reproduced or used in any manner without written permission of the copyright owner except for the use of quotations in a book review.

Cover design by info@amapopico.com and Book Cover Zone.

Map of Chalk Gap Village

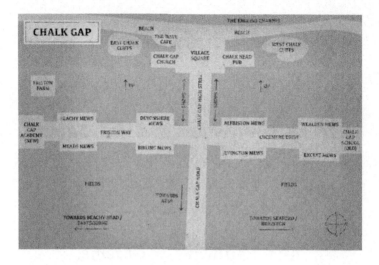

To my family: Mum and Dad, Karen and Steven. Thank you for all your support in helping me become who I am today, firmly out of the closet!

And, as always, to Graeme.

~~I've hidden who I am for 25 years.~~

~~25 years is a long time.~~

~~25 years is a long time to live with a secret like this.~~

~~I want to say who I really am.~~

~~I want to tell the world who I really am.~~

~~I want to tell the people who love me who I really am.~~

~~I'm just going to come out with it: I'm gay.~~

~~I'm gay. It's such a relief to be able to write these words.~~

I'm gay. And I'm a footballer. I'm a gay footballer.

NOTE DELETED

1

Watching football reminds me of 'playing' it in PE at school, when I was always the last one picked. I'd be standing shivering, sleeves dangling way past my arms in the borrowed kit that was far too big, watching the respective team captains look right through me: making their choices as if I wasn't there.

Apart from Jamie Appleby, my bully; whenever he captained, he'd flash his smug, arrogant grin at me as he passed me over. Then, when I was the last one left, he'd deliver the final blow.

'Come on then, Edward, looks like we're stuck with you. Don't worry mate, even you can't be worse than you were last time.'

I'd still hear the laughs of the whole PE class ringing in my ears as I stumbled around the muddy pitch, praying that the ball didn't come anywhere near me, literally counting the seconds to hear the whistle signifying the end of my 90 minutes of torture. And then spend the rest of the school day reliving my humiliation, waiting for the end of day bell to ring so I could retreat home into the world of reading murder mysteries. The only respite from the anxiety that lived in my heart.

I'd like to say a lot's changed since those days. Some things have, some haven't. I still love retiring into the lands of Sherlock Holmes, Poirot, Miss

Marple et al when I want to escape the world around me. And I still have crippling anxiety. But I cope with it a lot better, a lot of days. And my old school bully is now a Detective Inspector with Sussex Police CID, and I've assisted him in solving several real life murder cases using my *expertise*, as my mum calls it.

Would I still be picked last in a football team? I was pondering this as I stood, feeling out of place, watching Beachy Head United's private training session at their imaginatively titled home, Beachy Head Stadium.

I'll forgive you for not knowing it if you're not a football fan or from our area; the stadium is relatively new, as is the team's rapid rise to success in the last few years. A small local semi-pro team at first, a change of ownership to a billionaire businessman, Vincent Tan, saw Beachy Head United rocket through the leagues and become a Premiership football side, competing against the best football teams in the country.

Despite their home being just a mile or so from our village, Beachy Head United had barely touched my life up until now (yes, Dad is a huge fan and proudly shows all the games in our family's pub, but I avoid visiting on match days) so this was my first time visiting the stadium. The first thing I noticed was the sea of green and white, everywhere; the bright colours of the seats, the stands and the players' kits all represented the countryside of our beautiful South Downs.

Many of the players themselves were now genuine celebrities - loved and loathed online, gossiped about in the tabloids – and I could tell that this had gone to the heads of some players as I observed them train.

'Do that again, Roberts, see what happens!' I heard one player howl at another as he fell to the ground after a savage looking tackle.

'What you gonna do, Higgins?' the other player growled menacingly as he stood over him. 'You can't even keep your missus in check, let alone any of us.'

'Ricky Roberts is a nasty piece of work,' my best friend Patrick said from the seat next to me. 'If he's not fouling every other player, he's winding them up.'

I kept my eyes on the curly haired, tattooed player as he sauntered away from his fallen teammate. 'But why someone on his own team?'

Patrick was my football expert, I knew he would have more insight. But he didn't get a chance to tell me.

'Jealousy,' piped up my other best friend, Kat, from the opposite side of me. 'Danny Higgins and his girlfriend are bonafide celebrities. Twitter, Instagram, magazine deals... they're everywhere. That oaf who just fouled him? Not so much. I've no idea who he is.'

'She's right,' replied Patrick with a sigh. 'He is known but not as much outside football fans and the occasional kiss and tell. Anyway, Roberts hates Danny Higgins. But hold on, look. Higgins isn't taking it lying down.'

Sure enough, the younger, better looking player was back on his feet and storming after his assailant with a yell. 'Come here and say that to my face!'

'Gladly, mate,' Ricky Roberts said with a smirk as he stopped and faced him. 'Which one? Your real one, or the one you show all your *fans*?'

The two squared up to each other; this didn't look good: until a third player, one I recognised, shoved his way in between them. 'That's enough, lads. We're teammates, remember. Not to mention we have guests today. Now walk away.'

Both players turned away, Danny with a slight hobble as he walked.

'You okay, mate?' the third man asked him as he put his hand on his shoulder.

'Golden boy to the rescue of his boyfriend, what a shock,' Ricky Roberts quipped.

But *golden boy* wasn't having it. 'Oi, Roberts. I'm your captain, don't forget that.'

'Yes Kieron, of course, sorry,' Ricky replied with sarcasm I could spot all the way from my seat in the south stand.

The three men separated, and the training

session resumed. But I didn't know at that point that one of those three men would soon be murdered. And it would be the one I least expected, for a reason that would make history.

2

I've not even explained why the three of us were at the training session in the first place. Even though we socialise together (more socialising is another development for me in the last year), it isn't usually in empty stadiums watching millionaire footballers having a clash of egos.

We were representing our village school, Chalk Gap Academy, where Kat is the Head Teacher and Patrick is the English and PE teacher. Looking back, I can see why those two in their job roles were there that day, but I'm not sure why the school librarian got roped in. I was certain I'd looked visibly uncomfortable in the press photos we'd endured earlier. And I wasn't especially looking forward to the celebration reception that evening; I only had a few chapters left to read in my latest book, and I was excited to find out if I'd guessed the killer correctly. It would have to wait until tomorrow.

Having one of our sixth form students sign with Beachy Head United's first team was a great honour to both our school and village. It wasn't often that little Chalk Gap got much spotlight (beyond the recent murders), and it would do wonders for the reputation of Chalk Gap Academy. Kat was also especially proud because of the player being one of her family (actually, it was upon her invitation, so that was probably why I was there).

Beaumont Albright was the son of our local GP, Dr Beverley Albright, Kat's cousin. He'd played football from a young age and had been signed to a lower league youth team, but on turning 18 he'd got the attention of our local heroes and was Beachy Head United's brightest new signing.

The entire village was buzzing with excitement at the news. Dad had already christened our family's pub, The Chalk Inn, *the Official Pub of Beachy Head United* as soon as they were promoted to the Premier League, but as I arrived at the pub that evening ready to meet Kat for the celebration reception, I noticed a new sign: *Beaumont Albright drinks here.*

'Dad, no he doesn't! He's not even been 18 for very long.'

'His birthday was 2nd March, son. That's nine weeks he could have been drinking here for.' His voice sounded adamant as he 'fixed' the sign, probably for the twentieth time that day.

'And has he?'

'No, but he could have,' Mum chipped in. 'Besides, he came in with his mum for a Sunday lunch a couple of years ago. He had two glasses of lemonade then, so that's *drinks* plural.'

I suppressed a laugh as she continued. 'I bet Doctor Albright is chuffed to bits that her son's career is taking off like this. I just hope he stays the pleasant lad he's always been, and doesn't become like the rest of them. Honestly, brawling like that while you were watching.'

I knew I'd regret telling her about the incident in the training session. 'It was barely brawling, Mum. A couple of them just had words with each other.'

But she was off now. 'Words aren't the only things those lot have had. Up to all sorts, I've read. Their antics are always online and in the papers. Just watch out for them tonight when you're off gallivanting with these celebrities and missing our karaoke night.'

It was true that the press and social media were often buzzing with the off-pitch behaviour of the Beachy Head United players. As much as they'd brought attention to our little corner of the world, sometimes it was the wrong kind.

'And of course,' Mum started ominously as she appeared in front of me and began fixing my tie, 'there's *that* rumour about one of them.'

'Oh yes, Dad replied, nodding his head. '*That* rumour.'

As is often the case with my parents, I had no clue what they were talking about. 'What rumour?'

'You know,' Mum said, as she stepped back from tie-fixing to admire her handiwork. 'That one of them is...'

Not being able to say what she means wasn't one of her usual traits. 'Is what?'

'You know,' she repeated. I didn't know; that's

why I was having this frustrating conversation. 'The big rumour. That one of them is... on our Alfie's bus.'

Her mouthing of those last few words made this discussion even more ridiculous. Mum and Dad were so proud of my brother, I knew that for a fact, and didn't care about his sexuality.

'Gay, you mean? What's wrong with that?'

'Nothing, son, of course,' Dad said. 'Just that there aren't any openly gay players in football. Not in English Premier League football, anyway. A couple have come out after they've retired or gone to play elsewhere, but not while playing over here. Apparently they'd get too much trouble from the fans at other clubs.'

'Idiots! If someone wants to be gay and play football, good for them,' Mum declared, as she started fixing my tie yet again. 'But it is fun to speculate who it is, isn't it, Casper?'

'Mum, you don't even know who most of the players are.'

'No, but your dad does, don't you, Casper?' She barely gave him time to nod before she continued. 'He keeps me up to date with who's who. Besides, I read the internet.'

''My money's on Ricky Roberts, for the record,' Dad spoke up. 'He acts too macho, like he's over-compensating.'

'Especially after what you told us about

this afternoon,' Mum said, as I immediately regretted saying anything. 'He's definitely hiding something.'

'How do you know any of them are gay?' I asked. 'It's just a silly rumour, probably made up by the press.'

'It's true, the press does *sometimes* embellish the facts. But I'm going to be different when I'm a journalist.'

I turned to face Noah: my student library assistant, self-proclaimed partner in the murder cases I've solved, and now my foster brother. The first thing I noticed was that he was smartly dressed, in a grey suit, which looked much smarter than the shabby one I'd thrown on.

There's so much to say about Noah that I never know where to start when I mention him in these case notes. I guess I'll start with what he was talking about. His latest interest at the time was that he wanted to be a journalist. As you may remember, he has a deep fascination with murder mysteries, which hadn't gone away, but since becoming the editor of the school magazine, journalism had become all he talks about. Mum has been reading up about autism since the fostering, and keeps pointing out to me that fixated interests are common, but I don't even see it like that; it's just Noah being Noah.

That explains his comment about journalism; what I didn't have an answer for at the time was his attire. 'Noah, why are you dressed so smartly?'

He looked at me as if I'd asked the world's most stupid question. 'For the celebration reception, of course. I'm going undercover.'

I went to reply, but Mum got there first. 'Well, I think you look very handsome, my darling!'

'But, Noah, I'm afraid -'

Dad soon cut me off. 'Let the lad have his fun before you spoil it for him, son. Noah, what are you going under cover for?'

'An undercover journalist, of course!' Noah declared, oblivious to the exchange between me and Dad. 'You know, I was thinking about it - it's not too different from being an undercover detective. Except I'm not exposing a crime, but the Beachy Head players' deepest, darkest secrets!'

He said those last three words as dramatically as he could, with pauses in between, before looking at me for approval. I wasn't sure I had the heart to do this.

'I didn't realise you wanted to come, Noah. The thing is, it's strictly over 18s tonight.' It was probably for the best that it would spare Beachy Head United Noah's attempts at being Lois Lane, but the age limitation was correct: Beaumont himself was only nine weeks from being unable to attend his own celebration reception.

'Oh. Oh, yes of course.' He replied, but the disappointment I'd expected to be on his face wasn't there; instead, he simply reached into the jacket pocket of his suit. 'But I won't be drinking and I'll be there to work, so I don't think it matters. I have this.'

I glanced forward to see him holding out a laminated card dangling down from a lanyard and stating in large, bold red font: 'Press Pass.'

'What's this?' I asked, immediately realising my mistake with Noah, who answered every question literally.

'It's a press pass.' He placed the pass round his neck proudly, beaming as he did this. I refrained from saying that having a press pass on full display negated his undercover role, whatever it was.

I knew I needed to join the dots to find out. 'Yes, I can see it's a press pass, but why do you have it?'

He looked at me incredulously. Sometimes, Noah didn't realise that what was obvious to him needed explanation. 'I'm doing an unpaid internship with Fiona Turtle. For the Chalk Gap Observer.'

'The Observer, is that even still going?' Dad asked in between sips of his pint. 'I thought it shut down years ago.'

'Oh yes, Casper, it's very popular on social media. In fact, that's how I made contact with them.'

I was pretty sure that 'them' was just Fiona Turtle these days, who'd ran the Observer as an online only publication for the last few years. Fiona was very vocal on their social media pages, often getting into arguments with members of the public who commented on articles, having a bit of a reputation as a keyboard warrior. And she'd whipped up a bit of a stir online after the murder cases I'd solved, implying that Chalk Gap wasn't a safe place to live anymore.

Other than that, I didn't really know her, not anymore; she was in my brother's year at school and was briefly his girlfriend when they were around 16 (until Alfie realised he didn't like girls). I also remembered she was very shy, hurrying round everywhere with her head down and her green backpack pulled tightly to her. A specific memory suddenly came back to me: *Ninja Turtle*. That's what they used to call her as they laughed at her scuttling past. Maybe such abuse made her so handy behind her keyboard these days. But what had led her to Noah?

'How do you mean, made contact?'

'I commented on a few of the Observer's posts about local news items and Fiona often replied. She's really lovely, actually. Then I sent her a few private messages and we got talking, and she offered me an unpaid internship in between my college hours. Tonight is my first assignment!' He puffed himself up to look as tall as he could, once again grabbing his lanyard and thrusting it forward for us all to see.

'Well, I think it's wonderful, my love. I'm so proud of you!' Mum exclaimed, as she rushed forward and embraced him in a hug.

'What are you hoping to find out, exactly?' As I said this, I noticed an irrational pang of jealousy inside me and immediately felt guilty. Of course, like Mum, I was proud of Noah; he'd overcome so much already and constantly put himself out there in the world with no doubts or care for what anyone else thought. But when I was his age, I barely left the comfort of my bedroom and my own private library. Hell, I'd only just developed much beyond that in the last year. Lost in my thoughts, it took me a moment to realise that Noah had started answering my question.

'Fiona and I have a list of things to look out for,' he said as he pulled out his phone. Noah records absolutely everything in his Notes app; he's used it constantly throughout the murder cases we've been involved in and it must make for very interesting reading. But maybe not for the eyes of Beachy Head United. 'The club's alleged financial difficulties, rumours of a management restructure, the identity of the gay player... and, you might be able to help me with this one, talk of tension between the players. Wasn't there an incident between some players at the training session today?'

How on earth had Fiona Turtle heard about that so quickly? It was a private training session, and we were the only members of the public there. I doubted Patrick or Kat would have said anything, so that left someone from the club itself. But the Chalk Gap observer would soon have far more to report on than squabbles between the players. In fact, it would happen later that night.

3

'No way. No. way. Oh wow, is this really happening? Patrick, look at these name plates. *Chloe Stone. Danny Higgins. Ellie Marsden. Kieron Juniper.* As if they've sat us with the two biggest power couples in all of East Sussex. I can't see them yet, can you? Oh my god, I'm so under-dressed. As if I'm going to be sitting with Chloe Stone looking like this.'

I'd arrived at the celebration reception with Patrick and his girlfriend, Becky Lau, who was a Science teacher at our school. You would never know that from her behaviour at this moment, though; she was a full-on celebrity obsessed superfan.

'Relax, baby, they're just people,' Patrick reassured her. 'I've told you, when I was at school with Kieron's older brother, he was just a normal kid. He's an ordinary guy, from an ordinary family.'

'Don't get me started on that,' she retorted. 'How you've never wangled us an introduction to him and Ellie before now, I don't know. I wouldn't need to be so nervous if I'd met them already.'

Patrick and I shared an eye roll. 'I said before baby, he probably wouldn't even remember me, he was barely knee high.'

To be fair, any anxiety Becky had about sitting with celebrities, I had tenfold. Sure, I barely knew who these people were; funnily enough, I had little interest in either football or celebrity gossip. But I'd cultivated my social circle - now that I finally had one - carefully to only include people I was completely comfortable with. I even hated the thought of the old boys in the pub judging me when I visited Mum and Dad. I dreaded to think what bona fide famous people - actual good-looking, successful people - would make of me.

'Wow, look at everyone, they all look gorgeous!' Becky continued, as if to make my point. '*Hello* magazine would have a field day here. Patrick, do you think anyone will notice if I take a few photos? My Instagram followers will love this.'

'I told you, baby, we had to agree. No photos, no videos, no disclosure of anything we see here. Edward and I both had to sign something, you know that.'

'I can't wait to see what Chloe Stone is wearing, I bet it's something stunning. I was in love with the dress she wore at the Soap Awards last year. Her and Danny Higgins will look so good together, they always do.' I smiled politely as she continued to twitter on. 'Mind you, Ellie Marsden will look beautiful, too. She's a more natural beauty, though, as opposed to Chloe's look, which I guess is a bit more superficial.'

Patrick managed to get a word in as she finally stopped for breath. 'Baby, just be careful what you say, you never know who's listening.'

'What, who, where?' she said as she whipped

her head round to see if anyone was approaching the table. 'If Chloe heard me criticising her, I'd be mortified.'

I followed Becky's gaze round the room and noticed the grandness of everything: the chandeliers, the immaculately dressed servers pouring champagne, the ridiculously unidentifiable 'nibbles' on each table. It looked like a really expensive wedding, one where the amount of money spent far exceeds the level of taste. There must have been every colour of the rainbow on display in the outfits I could see, and that was just the men's suits.

It was then I noticed something that stood out among everything else. Something that didn't quite belong. Or should I say, *someone*. The lady I spotted had a bright red flower in her hair, and thick-framed glasses of the same colour. Her dress was white with red polka dots, along with a necklace of large white beads around her neck and a red woollen cardigan over her shoulders. Finally, as she moved closer, I saw a badge on her dress saying 'vintage vixen.' She stood out a mile among the fashion conscious, expensively dressed women, but it didn't look like she cared.

It was only as she neared our table I spotted who was behind her: Noah. Which meant that this 'vintage vixen' must be Fiona Turtle.

'Edward, it must be years!' she said in a high pitch squeal before she even reached me, a little too loudly than socially expected, so much so that people turned to look. No wonder she and Noah got on.

Speaking of Noah, he of course couldn't have someone talking louder than him. 'Edward, Edward, look who it is! I didn't realise you two knew each other.'

Ignoring the dirty looks from several people around us, I introduced Fiona to Patrick and Becky. As I did this, I noticed her eyeing up the nameplates of the empty seats on our table; no doubt the real reason she was so keen to come over.

'Ah, you've got Beaumont, our guest of honour, sat with you. They'll be announcing him in soon. But no sign of Kieron or Danny and their lady friends yet?' she asked, trying and failing to sound as casual as she could. But she didn't give us time to answer. 'Noah mentioned their little scuffle with Ricky Roberts earlier. I wondered if that's why they're missing. You were there, weren't you? What was it that happened?'

I suppressed a smile. Subtle she was not, in either journalistic approach or dress sense. And Noah hadn't even told her about it; in fact, he'd heard it from her. I made a mental note not to trust her. But, all the same, there was something about her I couldn't help but like.

'My Patrick was there, he told me all about it!' Becky said with excitement. 'Chloe hates bad publicity, doesn't she? I bet they've had an argument about it and that's why they're late.'

Fiona's eyes lit up. 'Becky, isn't it? Why don't we pop to the ladies' and you can tell me all about it?' She linked Becky's arm and led her away. But she hadn't counted on Noah.

'Oh, is this investigative journalism?' he called after them. 'I'll come with you.'

I pulled Noah back and explained the difference between ladies' and gentlemen's toilets and why he couldn't go with them.

Patrick looked worried. 'I hope Becky's okay, she's really naïve about people like Fiona. She'll be telling her our life stories.'

'Oh, Fiona has no interest in ordinary, boring people like you. She only wants to know about celebrities.'

'And Becky only knows what she's read on Twitter and the gossip columns, she'll be fine,' I reassured him quickly, hoping to distract him from the bluntness of Noah's comment.

I needn't have distracted him, as we soon had our attention drawn elsewhere.

'Ladies and gentlemen,' a vaguely familiar, gruff South London voice boomed across the room. 'I've been given the last minute honour of a very special responsibility.'

'For the first time in your life!' heckled one voice.

'Can you even tie your shoelaces, Roberts?'

Ricky Roberts, of course. I looked across the

room to see the man himself, microphone in hand, circling the centre of the room with a swagger and a cocky grin on his face. 'Yeah, alright lads, course I can tie my shoelaces. I can also turn up on time, unlike our precious Captain, which is why you're stuck with me.'

Kieron Juniper was definitely AWOL then; they obviously meant it to be him introducing the club's newest signing. And there was no sign of Danny Higgins, or either of their girlfriends. I'd not paid much attention to Fiona Turtle's stirring of trouble, but it was seeming something might be wrong.

As I considered this, I saw Kat making her way towards our table; she'd obviously waited with Beaumont until his grand introduction. Beaumont's mum, our village GP Dr Beverley Albright, had been called away to an emergency appointment so Kat was now pulling double duty representing their family and the school. She'd almost made it to our table; I could see she looked relieved to escape the attention of Roberts on the microphone.

Except she hadn't quite. 'Well, well, well, who do we have here? Ladies and gentlemen, the beautiful woman you can see standing across the room is Kat Parker, our brand new signing's glamorous auntie. And yes, I agree, she looks far too young to be Beaumont's auntie.'

That's because she isn't, I thought to myself as I

rolled my eyes. Her cousin's son would be her first cousin, once removed. How did he even know her name, though? And what was this, an attempt to impress her? His teammates seemed to think so.

'Go on, Roberts!' one heckling voice shouted.

'Bet you wish you'd got a haircut, you scruffy sod!' said another.

'Just my luck, it's due tomorrow. You never know when you're gonna run into a beautiful lady.'

This guy was something else. I cringed for Kat as he continued.

'Kat is also the Head Teacher of Chalk Gap Academy, the school which has done such a fine job of educating Beaumont. A local treasure, the Beyoncé of the teaching world.'

I saw Kat's embarrassment at his cringeworthy words; she would hate that. It was hard to tell if he was being genuine or sarcastic; he sounded insincere with everything he said. But she would definitely hate the cliched racial comparison. 'And speaking of Beaumont, let's talk about the reason we're all here.'

As Roberts talked a little about Beaumont's history, Kat sat down next to me. 'Can you believe him, Ed? Especially the Beyoncé thing, what an idiot.'

I smiled at Kat calling me 'Ed': the only person who could get away with calling me that. Mainly because I daren't ever tell her otherwise. If Ricky

Roberts thought she would be an easy notch on his bedpost, he was in for a shock.

'This is what Roberts is like,' Patrick whispered from my other side. 'He's after Kat to get one over on the newest member of the team. What better way to wind young Beaumont up than say he's pulled his auntie?'

'That's right, it's all about power with him, he's done this kind of thing to lots of players,' I heard a voice across the table as Fiona returned with Becky and took one of the empty seats next to her. 'What? It doesn't seem like they're coming anytime soon, so these seats are free.'

'Shush everyone, it's time!' Noah said, as he took one of the other empty seats.

'And without further ado, let me introduce the man of the moment. Our latest signing, and the future of our club... ladies and gentlemen, may I present, Beaumont Albright!'

The entire room rose to its feet and applauded as the eighteen-year-old appeared in a sharp turquoise suit and pink tie, a nervous smile on his face. I heard a couple of wolf whistles and wondered if they were from female admirers or sarcastic teammates. A table of older men in grey suits and glasses of whiskey in front of them looked very pleased with themselves; they were probably the club's management and Directors' board. A plump, short, middle-aged lady in a trouser suit cheered loudly as I wondered who she was: not a relative of Kat's family, as far as I knew.

'He's dreamed of this as long as I can remember,' Kat said. 'I'm so proud of him.'

I glanced across the table and shared a look with Fiona Turtle. I imagined she was thinking the same as me, hoping that this football club would look after this young man, and not chew him up and spit him out.

'And now, main man,' Roberts continued on the microphone with a smirk on his face, 'let's not keep your audience waiting any longer, shall we? Time for you to say a few words.'

I saw momentary panic flash across Beaumont's face as Roberts held the microphone out. This clearly hadn't been planned, and the older man was trying to catch him out. But before Beaumont could step forward, the plump lady leapt from her chair and shot forward.

'Jackie Luton, Beaumont's agent,' Fiona whispered across the table. 'Most of the club's agent, actually.'

Before she could reach the microphone, another woman entered the room, pushing Beaumont out of her way in the doorway. Roberts looked confused, and Jackie Luton looked horrified as she stalked towards them.

'Ellie Marsden!' Fiona and Becky chorused in excitement at our table.

'Kieron Juniper's girlfriend?' I asked out loud.

'We're going to get a scoop!' Noah called out as Fiona took her phone from her handbag and started recording.

By this time, Ellie had reached the centre of the room and ripped the microphone out of Ricky Roberts' hand. I saw her face properly for the first time; she'd been crying, her make-up was running, and she'd clearly had a few drinks. She looked around the room, suddenly scared, as if realising what she'd done and that she didn't actually know what to say.

'Come on, love, give me that,' Jackie Luton said gently to her, reaching her hand out. There was a moment's silence as Ellie considered her.

'You'd like that, wouldn't you? You'd all like that.' She glared across at the management table. 'I bet you knew already, didn't you? I bet you all knew and kept it quiet, for the sake of your club.'

'Knew what?' said Roberts, with mischief on his face.

'What he really is, what he's been all along,' she spat out with absolute venom. 'What he's used me to cover up this whole time.'

'Ellie, no!' two loud voices shouted from the doorway. We all looked to see Chloe Stone and Danny Higgins standing there. Kieron himself was nowhere to be seen.

'No, it's too late,' she snapped back at them. 'I'm not keeping it a secret for him after what he's done to me, no way.'

'Kieron been playing away, has he?' Roberts said with a cruel laugh.

'I don't know, probably,' she answered through the microphone. 'But if he has, it's not with a girl. I've just found out that Kieron, this club's beloved Kieron, has been hiding in the closet.'

The room fell into stunned silence.

'Yes, that's right,' she went on. 'Kieron Juniper is gay.'

4

Nothing happened for a few seconds. I could tell that Ellie's actions weren't planned; she'd dropped her bombshell to the whole room and now had no idea what to do next.

I should have guessed who'd break the silence.

'Edward, Kieron Juniper can't be gay, can he? Ellie is his girlfriend, wouldn't she mind?'

There were several sniggers from players sitting near us, with one of them muttering, 'I'd say it looks like she minds, little buddy.'

'So, it's his royal highness, King Juniper batting for the other side, is it?' Roberts sneered. 'He's the reason we've had all those press rumours about one of us being on the wrong bus. It was our skipper all along.'

Meanwhile, Jackie Luton took charge of the floor show. 'Nothing to see here folks, just a drunk girlfriend talking rubbish she won't even remember in the morning,' she barked as loud as she could. Everyone looked away quickly, obeying a command she hadn't even given. This woman didn't need a microphone to be heard.

'Danny, get her out of here, now,' I heard her say to Danny Higgins, though this was much quieter and not meant for everyone's ears.

'Come on, hun, let's get some fresh air,' Chloe Stone said gently, putting her arms round her while Danny took the microphone off her.

Ellie, who hadn't spoken for several moments, didn't like this. 'Chloe, what are you doing? Don't try and shut me up. You're the one who told me!'

'So it came from your missus, did it, Danny? What are we gonna find out next, are you his secret boyfriend?'

'Say that again. I dare you,' Danny said, squaring up to Roberts.

'It all makes sense now,' Roberts continued with glee. 'I'm curious though… which one of you is the woman?'

Several players jumped out of their seats now, making a beeline for the two just in time as Danny hurled himself towards Roberts.

Jackie Luton stepped forward and immediately took charge. 'Lads, get Danny out of here. Roberts, take young Beaumont to the bar and get him the most expensive drink you can. On you. As an apology for your part in spoiling his big night.'

'MY part? I'm not the one who…'

'Roberts,' she repeated firmly, not taking her eyes off him.

'Yes, boss,' Roberts sighed. 'Come on, youngster, let's see what you're made of then.'

As Roberts led Beaumont to the bar and Danny had safely been escorted away, Jackie turned to the women.

'Chloe, get her out of here. And I'll speak to you

later,' she said ominously.

'Jackie, about me telling her...'

'Look, I can see it's just a rumour between you girls. I know what it's like when there's arguments with your boyfriends and there's alcohol involved. But we can't have people thinking it's true about Kieron,' she said pointedly, obviously wanting people to hear.

'It IS true about Kieron!' Ellie screamed, as everyone watched round two. 'You think we've made this up? Yes, Chloe told me, but he admitted it himself, just now. I even saw the draft coming out statement he's written!'

'Chloe. Get her out, now,' Jackie said once more, in a tone that was attempting authority but sounded absolutely petrified. Finally, Chloe led Ellie out, with a couple of other women joining her to help, or more likely, attempt to get the gossip.

'That's it, the show's over,' Jackie barked once more as the room finally got back to normal.

'What a scoop!' Noah exclaimed, looking delighted.

'What do we all make of that?' Becky asked, probably ecstatic to witness first-hand an episode of her favourite real life WAG soap opera.

'You do all realise that if what she said is true,' Patrick started before pausing for emphasis, 'this is a game changer for English football. An openly gay premiership footballer is unheard of. We've probably just witnessed history.'

'And I have it all recorded, word for word,' Fiona said as she waved her phone in the air.

'I don't think so, love,' I heard someone say before I fully comprehended what was happening. By the time I realised what was happening, Jackie Luton was standing behind Fiona, in possession of the phone. 'I'll take that, thank you.'

'You can't do that, that's mine. Give it back!' Fiona squawked awkwardly, attempting to grab the phone in vain.

'I think I can,' Jackie replied sternly. 'You know the rules. You signed the agreement, press or not. No photo or video footage to be taken, and certainly not to be released to the public, which I assume is what you intend.'

'Of course that's what I intend, did you see that? This is going to be world news tomorrow. You can't stop me telling what we saw, this is my story.'

'There is no story, Turtle. Just a drunk, bitter WAG making up a silly lie to get back at her boyfriend because they've had an argument.' She spoke slowly and deliberately; she was definitely used to people doing as they were told when she spoke.

But Fiona wasn't going down without a fight. 'If that's all it is, there's no harm in me having my phone back, is there?'

'I'm sorry,' Jackie retorted in a falsely sweet

voice. She wasn't sorry. 'Your device will be available to collect from the club reception desk in 48 hours.'

'When my footage will no doubt have been wiped.'

'That's a strong accusation to make against a football club with an excellent legal team,' Jackie replied as she walked away, triumphant. 'Have a good evening, Miss Turtle.'

'Sorry you lost your footage, boss,' Noah said. I wasn't sure quite when he'd started calling Fiona 'boss' but she was probably stuck with it for life now.

'It's not over yet,' Fiona said as she got to her feet. 'There are two girls out there who know the story and I'm going to get it. Come on, Noah.'

'I'll come too,' Becky said quickly, before Patrick could object. She was having the time of her life, and he probably couldn't have stopped her if he tried.

'I'm just going to check Beaumont is alright with that idiot,' Kat announced as she stood up, leaving just me and Patrick at the table.

'Poor Kieron, I hope he's alright,' Patrick said with a look of sadness in his eyes, as he poured us both a glass of wine from the bottle on the table.

'Do you think it's true?'

'I've no idea, buddy. I barely knew him as a kid, he's seven or eight years younger than me and his brother. But as a footballer, he's one of the most respected in the game, both as a player and a man. He's taken this team to new heights, not just with the goals he's scored but with his leadership too.' He stopped and took a big gulp of his wine. His words were fairly positive, but he looked worried.

'So he'll get a lot of support then, surely?' I ventured, flinching as I followed suit and swallowed the dry, strong alcohol. I wouldn't normally drink wine without choosing it carefully, but it didn't seem the right situation to object.

'I don't know. Like I said, this is a game changer. There are *no* openly gay players in professional football in this country. You really think there aren't any?'

'Statistically it's unlikely,' I agreed as I moved my wine glass a few more inches safely away from me.

'Exactly, buddy. Of course there are. There must be. And why haven't they come out? There's been lots of debate: that the opposition fans would be too toxic at the games and on social media, that they would use it against them, that the football world is too masculine to deal with it. But there's also many people who say, come on, it's the twenty-first century, it would be fine. Apparently, quite a few players are privately out to their teammates and clubs, and are well supported.' He paused again. I knew football was one of Patrick's biggest passions, and he obviously cared about the social issues surrounding it too.

'He should be okay, then,' I said, in retrospect quite naively. 'You never know, he might already be out to some of the team.'

He scoffed. 'Edward, that didn't look like a room of people in the know. Danny Higgins, probably. But even that seemed like a recent revelation. And you've got idiots like Ricky Roberts on the team, and an agent and club who clearly want to brush it under the carpet. I feel for the guy: he's going to need support.'

I thought about it. Alfie and I have loving, supportive, wonderful parents who couldn't have reacted better to his coming out, but even so he's always said it's the hardest thing he's ever had to do. But this wasn't just coming out to loved ones, this was coming out to the entire world. When you maybe weren't even ready to. It was then an idea came to me. 'What are we waiting for?'

Patrick stared at me as he downed the last of his wine, thankfully not noticing I'd barely touched mine. 'What are you talking about?'

'Ellie went off with Chloe and the rest of the WAGS, and Danny got carted off to calm down. But no one's mentioned the person this is all about: Kieron. Ellie said he'd just spoken to her outside the room. So where is he?'

'Edward, buddy, you're brilliant,' he said, as he picked up my leftover wine and downed it in one. 'Let's see if he remembers his brother's old friend.'

5

Kieron wasn't too difficult to find. Logic suggested that he'd want to hide from Ellie right now, so the obvious theory was he'd be somewhere she couldn't go.

'The private VIP toilets are stuff of legend at Beachy Head Stadium,' Patrick explained after we'd ducked the barrier as we climbed up the steep, red velvet stairs. 'So many supporters have tried and failed on match days to break into them.'

'Why's that?' I questioned, puzzled. 'Surely the dressing rooms are more popular.'

'Yeah, but there's no chance of getting anywhere near them. The private toilets are here in the main building, where there's few people around during the game apart from a few bar staff. There's even a social media challenge to break in and leave a message on the cubicle for your favourite player. #BeachyBoysBogBreak-in.'

'It's a good job you don't take Becky to the games with you, she'd be breaking into the ladies' to leave messages for the WAGS,' I said as I tried to get my breath at the top of the stairs.

'Honestly, the level of fandom you get is crazy, buddy. Especially since we got into the Premier League a couple of years ago. These guys are superstars. That's why I'm worried about the spotlight that's going to be on Kieron.'

'Let's see if we can find him,' I said, as I went

to push the giant gold-plated door in front of me. Just as I did, the door pulled itself away from me and a young man with a bleached blonde crew cut and a pierced nose appeared in our path. He looked surprised to see us and didn't know what to do for a second.

'Sorry, we're in your way,' I mumbled as I stepped to one side.

'No problem,' he said, as he smiled dubiously and rushed down the stairs.

'Come on, let's get in quickly, before anyone else sees us. We're not meant to be up here, remember,' Patrick said as he gently nudged me forward.

'That was a player, then?' I asked.

'I didn't recognise him, but he's probably a reserve or an under 21.'

As we entered the room, I realised that the golden door was just the start of it. Everything in sight appeared to be gold-laden: sinks, taps, mirrors, even the urinals were gold. I felt like I'd climbed the beanstalk and found the golden goose.

My feet sank into the soft luxury carpet beneath me as I adjusted to the gold and took in the rest of my surroundings. The sink area contained more men's toiletries and aftershaves than I'd perhaps ever seen, all luxury brands that I'd never even heard of.

The main room itself was spacious, with a gigantic black velvet sofa at its centre, with a life-size statue of what I guessed was an old player towering over it. I also noticed several gold doors leading to other areas: showers, bathing, sauna, tanning booth, bedroom. I didn't want to know what went on in that last one.

'How the other half live, eh?' Patrick said, as he looked around in awe. 'And this is just the toilets, I dread to think what other perks they get.'

'There seems to be no sign of him.' I could see four large cubicles, two on each side of the room, that all looked the size of a small room. They all seemed empty with no feet in view, but Patrick and I knew better than that, exchanging a glance. I certainly knew how to hide in cubicles from all my experience of escaping bullies at school.

Patrick nodded at me, and when he spoke it was in a gentle voice. 'Kieron, I know you're there, mate. I want to help you.'

'Sod off, whoever you are. You're not meant to be in here.'

'I'm used to being in places I'm not meant to, buddy. I got that from your brother. From Anthony.'

There was silence for a second. 'Who is... wait, Patrick? Patrick Herrera? Is that you?'

'Yes, it's me, buddy. I'm here for you.'

We saw two shiny, expensive black leather shoes drop to the floor one at a time in one of the cubicles, followed by the sound of a door unlocking.

I mentioned earlier that I vaguely recognised Kieron, and on the pitch in the training session he seemed a larger-than-life presence. But as he faced us now, in these bizarre golden toilets, coming out of hiding, he looked different. His eyes were red; had he been crying? His mop of hair was a mess and his crumpled shirt was open down to the first three buttons. But when he smiled at Patrick - a defeated, reluctant smile–I saw a flash of the charm that had won everyone over. Until now.

'Patrick, everything's messed up,' he said as he blinked back tears. Patrick later said that it was like seeing the seven-year-old boy again that Kieron was when he last saw him.

'It's okay, buddy,' Patrick said, before Kieron threw himself forward and hugged him. 'Why don't you tell me and Edward all about it.'

Patrick introduced me and we all sat down together on the huge velvet sofa, which still seemed to have lots of space despite having three adult men on it.

'I know you,' Kieron muttered through sniffles as he looked at me. 'You're the amateur detective guy. The one who's solved the local murders. I might be able to use your brain on this one.'

'Oi, what about my brain?' Patrick joked as he gently punched Kieron's arm.

'If you had a brain, you wouldn't have been

mates with my brother,' he replied with a laugh before pausing. 'Seriously though, it's good to see you, mate, after all these years. I'm glad you're here. I need someone.'

'You've got Danny, though, right?' Patrick said, steering the conversation to the matter in hand.

I thought I saw a flash of anger across Kieron's face. 'It's all a load of bull... everyone here. It's not real.'

I considered his words. My guess was that Danny had learned his secret in confidence, then betrayed his trust to Chloe, who told Ellie.

Patrick was evidently thinking along the same lines. 'Did Danny break your trust by telling Chloe, buddy?'

Kieron exhaled noisily before answering. 'You could say that. But it doesn't matter now. It's out there.'

Patrick and I glanced at each other but didn't speak, waiting to see if he'd continue unprompted. He didn't.

'That you're gay?' Patrick asked gently. Silence again. 'Kieron, you can tell us or not tell us anything you like, it's totally your call. But I just want you to realise that because of what Ellie said, a version of the truth is going to circulate, whether or not it's accurate. Like you said, it's out there.'

I was trying to read the expression on Kieron's face, but it wasn't easy. I couldn't even imagine what he was going through. I thought back to all those years ago, psyching Alfie up to tell Mum and Dad. But here, the decision to come out had been taken out of his hands. Not to mention, he was a household name who was coming out to millions of people in unprecedented territory for his career, with no idea how the world would react.

'Yeah, what Ellie said, it ruined everything,' he finally said. 'But it's not her fault. I can't blame her. She only acted on what Chloe told her. I need to talk to her. Explain what's going on.'

'And what *is* going on?' Patrick asked.

'The biggest dilemma of my life,' he replied. 'And I've no idea what I'm supposed to do. Do you stay true to who you are, or go through with a lie for the sake of someone else?'

I felt guilt for the relief to me that this was Patrick's old friend, not mine. I wouldn't have a clue what to advise.

'It's a tough one, buddy,' Patrick offered. 'No matter how difficult it is, be true to yourself, I guess.'

'I know you're right,' Kieron agreed. 'I have to be true to myself. Even if it damages someone else. But that's what I'm afraid of.'

And with that, he stood up and walked out of the room.

6

No one quite knew how to carry on for the rest of the evening. Technically, it was still the celebration reception for Beaumont's signing, but the drama with Ellie and Kieron had put a definite dampener over the party.

According to Kat, Jackie Luton had given the whole room a strict talking to, stating clearly that any word about it outside of those four walls would find the perpetrators with legal action from the club and / or a severe fine, depending on if they were a player, employee, family member or member of the press. I doubted how successful the warning would be in our current social media age, but I hoped for Kieron's sake that it would be: at least until he had time to think about what he wanted and talk to Ellie.

Despite the looming threat of legal action, the club's Board had also insisted that everyone must have a good time in Beaumont's honour and had put unlimited funds behind the bar.

Somehow, Fiona Turtle had persuaded Chloe Stone, Danny's girlfriend, to join us at our table; apparently they were 'frenemies' who had a loose friendship of convenience, where they used each other respectively for titbits of WAG news (Fiona's benefit) and exclusive coverage when needed (Chloe's benefit). Right now they were both dominating the conversation at our table, earning the occasional evil eye from a suspicious Jackie across the room.

Becky was, of course, sitting in between them, loving every moment of her new celebrity connections, much to Patrick's chagrin. She also seemed to have had a little too much to drink.

'I really feel like I've made two best friends for life!' she squealed as she put her arm round both the journalist and the footballer's girlfriend (she'd told us she was a beauty influencer but I refuse to state that as her profession). 'And Chloe, you'll definitely follow me back on Instagram as soon as you can recharge your phone?'

'Yes, of course, sweetie,' Chloe replied in as false a tone I can remember hearing for a long while. 'The battery's just dead for tonight, that's all.'

'Oh, that's strange. I definitely saw you use it just two minutes ago,' Noah announced loudly across the table, earning a thunderous look from Chloe.

'Are you sure about getting the erm, special needs boy to help you?' I heard her say in a low voice to Fiona once she thought no one could hear her. 'He seems sweet enough but he may be bad for your job.'

'I'm so sorry if he's upset you, Chloe,' I heard Fiona whisper back. I felt a flash of annoyance but supposed that Fiona needed to stay on the good side of people like Chloe for the good of her job. But she wasn't done. 'Though he's not going anywhere.

He's got a good nose for a story and his blunt honesty unsettles people who aren't ready to give us the full story, which I like.'

The look on Chloe's face was priceless. As she made an excuse and stomped away to a table with Danny and a few others on, Fiona caught my eye and gave a wink. 'She wasn't telling me anything interesting anyway, she's keeping her cards close to her chest.'

'You're not really friends with her, then?' I asked, though the answer was clear already. Fiona had clearly been cozying up to Chloe for the last hour to find out what she knew about Kieron's secret.

'Ha, of course I'm not!' she said with a wicked laugh. 'It's just what it's like with us, she knows the game.'

'So, you won't have a worldwide exclusive tomorrow then?'

'With Jackie Chan back there threatening to lawyer up, not likely,' she replied. 'Shame, this could be the biggest story ever. Though it still might be.'

I could see the mischief in her eyes. 'This is his life, Fiona. It could destroy him.'

'Relax, I don't know what kind of monster you think I am,' she snapped, her tone changing now. 'Ellie apparently said something about him admitting it, and she'd seen a draft coming out statement or something. I'd only publish if he was wilfully coming out, anyway.'

My cheeks reddened as I felt my usual deep embarrassment in situations like this. 'Ah, sorry.'

'Believe me,' she said, softening a little. 'I know what this business is like, and you're right. If he wasn't ready for it, they could destroy him.'

'Thanks, Fiona,' I said with a smile. 'And thanks for taking a chance on Noah, it's doing wonders for him.'

'Enough of this soppy crap, Edward Crisp, before you make me blush,' she joked. 'Actually, I need to go soon, I think my boss wants me to go cover a crash at Beachy Head.'

'I thought you *were* the boss?' I was sure she was the editor of the Chalk Gap Observer.

'I am, but we belong to the regional newspaper group. They can contact me pretty much 24/7 to cover something locally,' she said, before pausing. 'I'll take Noah with me in fact, he'll like that.'

As she spoke, I spotted Danny walk away from his table and leave the function room. Patrick and I exchanged a nod, and we stood up to follow him as we'd previously agreed.

We spotted him in the foyer outside, texting on his phone. Patrick made his approach.

'Excuse me buddy, sorry to disturb you,' he said politely and with his charming smile.

'Yes mate, can I help you?' Danny said

distractedly, only half looking up.

'Firstly, big fan of yours, it's an honour to meet you. But that's not why I'm speaking to you. My name is Patrick, I'm an old friend of Kieron's. Well, his brother actually, but anyway I spoke to him earlier. He was a bit upset.'

Danny whipped his head up instantly from his phone. 'You saw Kieron? When, where? No one's been able to find him all night. I can't get hold of him.'

'We saw him in the toilets, an hour or so ago. He was devastated. Weight of the world on his shoulders.' He stopped for a second and must have realised he'd not introduced me. 'Sorry, this is my friend, Edward.'

'Nice to meet you, mate,' Danny said, giving us both a firm handshake before turning back to Patrick. 'How did he seem, what else did he say?'

'Not a lot, just that he had a big dilemma,' Patrick replied. 'Look, it's not my business, but whatever happens now, he needs you.'

'I know he does.' I could see the concern on Danny's face as he spoke. 'This is all my fault.'

'I don't know what happened and I don't need to know, but if this is true it was a ticking time-bomb waiting to go off,' Patrick consoled him.

'Even if the story got to Ellie through you and your girlfriend, you weren't responsible for the big public scene she made,' I added.

'Yes, that's between them and he's obviously hurt her, but no one should be forced to come out before they're ready,' Patrick said.

'Thanks, guys,' Danny said with a smile. 'It's all such a mess. This is going to be national news if it isn't already. He doesn't deserve it.'

'No, then he's going to need you, buddy,' Patrick said. 'Go and find him.'

'He's probably driving round the Downs, he does that when he needs to clear his head,' Danny replied.

A terrible thought struck my mind. 'Wait a minute, what did you say?'

'I said he drives round the Downs to clear his head. Why?'

'And he was driving tonight?' I asked in a panic. 'Was he?'

'Yes, why, what's going on? Has something happened?' Danny asked with urgency now.

'Edward, what is it?' Patrick asked.

'It might be nothing,' I started, though I knew in my heart it wasn't. 'But Fiona Turtle just told me there's been a car crash at Beachy Head.'

7

We all looked at each other as realisation dawned on us.

'No, no, no, no,' Danny repeated in a horrified, hurried whisper. I could see the terror on the poor man's face, and hoped that he wouldn't have a full-blown panic attack. I allowed myself a release of breath as I remembered that my own were never too far away.

'It's okay, we don't know anything,' Patrick said, taking charge of the situation. 'But we need to get there. Danny, do you have your car?'

'No, Kieron drove us all, I've been drinking,' he blurted.

Luckily, I had an idea. 'It's okay, I know who can take us. But we have to be quick.'

'Fiona, wait!' I bellowed across the car park as we all ran towards where she and Noah were getting into her car.

'Oh my god, what is it?' she asked as we reached her and I tried to remember how to breathe properly. I explained between pants and the three of us jumped into the back seat.

'What else do you know, tell us!' Danny shouted, crammed in next to me behind Fiona (I was squashed in the middle seat, as I always seem to be when there's three people in the back of a car). He grabbed the back of her seat as he addressed her.

'Nothing much, I told Edward,' she replied, as I noticed her calm tone. 'Just that there's been a car crash at Beachy Head.'

We'd turned out of the stadium onto Warren Hill Road and had just passed the junction which turned into Beachy Head Road, leading to the famous cliffs themselves.

'We've come the same way Kieron would have driven,' Noah said. 'The junction would have been a potential site for a crash, but obviously we've just passed there. Therefore, the next most likely place is the bend before the cliffs where the Beachy Head pub is on the right.'

I saw the look on Danny's face and knew what he was thinking about the mention of the cliffs. Noah's logic was impressive, though; following this route, it was the next most likely place for the crash. In fact, he wasn't even a driver yet, but had still worked out a likely scenario. And he hadn't made an inappropriate, cringeworthy comment, either.

'Yes! I was right, I knew it was going to be here!' Maybe I'd spoken too soon.

Sure enough, a few hundred metres later, we met the police cordon and couldn't go any further. Even though it was dark, I could see a hive of activity: professionals of several fields all working together in what was clearly a major incident.

Danny jumped out of the car and ran towards the cordon, and before I realised what was happening, everyone had followed suit.

'What is this, what's happening?' Danny called out to the first uniformed officer.

'Who are you lot, the Scooby Gang?' the officer replied. To be fair, the five of us running towards him must have looked a sight.

'Chalk Gap Observer,' Noah said, stepping forwards proudly before anyone else had a chance to say anything.

The officer looked across the group incredulously before stopping at Fiona. 'Oh, it's you. Well, we can't release any information to the press, you'll have to wait.'

Danny stepped forward. 'No, you don't understand, I'm'

The officer took him in. 'Oh wait, I know you, you're...'

I saw his expression change as the penny dropped. 'Oh. Oh, I see. So, it must be him then. I knew he had a flash motor like that, and one witness claimed it was him.'

'Must be who? Kieron? Was it? Is it Kieron Juniper who's had the crash? Tell me! And where is he? I can't see his car anywhere?' Danny's barrage of questions hit the police officer one after the other.

I could tell the officer was considering what he could say. 'I'm really sorry, Danny. I can't tell you anything, it's more than my job's worth.'

'Edward!' I looked over to see who was calling me: it was PC Wood, now DC Wood. Dean Wood was from our village and I helped him in the snow day case when the rest of the police force couldn't get through. I excused myself from the group and went further along the cordon to meet him.

'I bet you're wondering why I'm at an accident scene now I'm a DC,' he said as I reached him.

I wasn't, but was polite. 'Yes, what are you doing here?'

'Uniform were short on numbers so they sent me, plus we don't know the circumstances yet, it might end up coming to our team, anyway.' That didn't sound good. 'What are you all doing here?'

'We were at a function at the stadium. We heard about this and were worried it might be someone from there. We've got Danny Higgins with us.'

Wood looked in recognition, but otherwise didn't make a fuss. 'Ah, it *is* Kieron Juniper then.'

'What's him, what's happened?' I asked. 'If he was in the crash, where's his car?'

Wood's face changed, and I realised what was coming. 'I'm really sorry, Edward. Kieron went straight over the edge of Beachy Head in his car. Coastguard is still working down there but he's almost certainly dead.'

8

It was after midnight when we got home to find Becky, Kat and Beaumont sitting in the kitchen waiting for us. Becky often stayed over with Patrick; Kat and Beaumont had travelled back with her and waited to see what further news we had. Fiona had driven us all home and dropped us off. Noah was also still with us; we'd tried to drop him back at Mum and Dad's but he insisted on coming to our house in case he missed anything, though he'd immediately gone into the living room by himself, saying he needed to work on something.

'Patrick!' Becky cried as she threw herself towards him and hugged him tight. Kat busied herself making drinks for everyone, while I noticed Beaumont looked particularly shaken.

'You doing okay, buddy?' Patrick asked him as he freed himself from Becky and patted the young footballer on the shoulder. Patrick ran the school football team and I remembered the two had a good relationship.

'I've always looked up to him. Even before tonight. He's the reason I wanted to play for this team.' This was a lot for an eighteen-year-old to deal with. Being thrust into the spotlight so young was trying enough, but having his role model die on what was the biggest night of his own career was not something he could have ever expected. Not to mention the drama that happened before that. Whether or not that information would become public, Beaumont and the entire team were sure to garner widespread media attention either way.

'And you'll be able to honour him by having a brilliant career,' Kat said as she put a steaming cup of tea in front of him. 'But for now, it's okay just to grieve him.'

'Thanks, Auntie Kat,' he said, as he put his hands round the hot cup before pausing ominously. 'Do you think it was an accident then?'

The question hung in the air for a few seconds, as if no one dare answer it. It seemed very unlikely to be an accident. No other vehicles or people had been involved, and two witnesses coming out of The Beachy Head pub had seen the car go off the road onto the embankment and straight over the edge of the cliff.

'We'll have to wait and see what the police say,' Kat said quietly.

We'd stayed for a couple of hours at the police cordon before we got moved on once more senior officers had arrived. DC Wood had kept checking in with us during that time but had little other news other than the basic details. The coastguard search and rescue team had apparently recovered a body but would be working long into the night on the car, and the body wouldn't be formally identified until tomorrow.

'I've got some information to share with you

all,' I heard from the hallway before Noah even entered the kitchen. Noah had been silent while we were waiting in Fiona's car, engrossed in reading on his phone, then every so often switching to his Notes app to write something. I guessed that this was what he'd gone into the living room to finish working on.

'What's that, Noah?' I asked, unsure what the answer was going to be.

'I was really intrigued about the news of Kieron Juniper being gay, even before the crash,' he started as he took a seat at the table. 'Especially with him having a girlfriend and everyone seeming so shocked. So I started researching the history of gay footballers.'

Oh dear. 'Maybe we should leave this for another time, we've had a long day.'

'No,' Beaumont said, putting his hand up. 'I'd like to hear it. It might be an interesting distraction.'

'Yeah, it's an interesting topic,' Patrick added. 'It's quite a short list, though, isn't it, Noah?'

'Yes, it is,' he confirmed, clearing his throat and picking his phone up, ready to read from. 'Firstly, we have Robbie Rogers; an American who played for Leeds United, but only came out in 2013 after a brief retirement. He played again in his home country of the US but never again over here once he was openly gay. Similarly, there's Thomas Hitzlsperger, a German player who appeared for various Premier League teams, but only came out in 2014 after his retirement.'

Patrick nodded in recognition at the names, while Beaumont listened intently. Kat and I exchanged a look, neither of us knowing who these men were. Noah continued.

'Liam Davis is the only current player on the list. He also came out in 2014 and still plays football, but it's at semi-professional level for lower league teams. And most recently, Thomas Beattie: an English footballer but played for teams in Canada and Singapore, he came out after retirement.'

'Is that everyone?' Beaumont asked.

No, not everyone,' Patrick said ominously.

'Justin Fashanu was a famous footballer in the 80s and 90s who played for various top flight football clubs, but before the current Premier League was formed. He came out midway through his career and was the first and currently only player in the UK to be openly gay while still playing top flight football.'

I recognised the name and felt like I vaguely knew his story. I had a feeling it didn't have a happy ending.

'Unfortunately, he lost his life to suicide after several personal troubles, it wasn't directly linked to his sexuality,' Patrick added gently. He jumped in quickly, probably before Noah could tell us in a possibly less diplomatic way.

It didn't seem to make a difference to Beaumont's reaction. He looked like he'd seen a ghost. Without saying a word, he got up and walked out of the room.

'I'll go after him,' Kat said, as she followed him.

'I can't believe there's no successful examples of players coming out and continuing to play professional football here while being openly gay,' Noah said. I could tell he was only just considering this. Noah liked facts and evidence, but often he would gather it first, then process it later.

'I can believe it,' Patrick said sadly. 'This is what I mentioned before, Edward. This is how it's always been. I think it says a lot about where we are in the sport and what we need to do. But, the frustrating thing is...'

He tailed off before he said anything more. 'What were you going to say?' I asked.

'No, it seems insensitive when the guy's just lost his life,' he continued. 'But I was going to say the frustrating thing is, we'll never know now. Because I have a feeling, if he *was* gay and he'd have come out openly, it would have been fine. More than fine, actually. The sport needs a gay role model like Kieron. He would have been fantastic. But now we'll never know.'

'Maybe we aren't meant to know,' Noah said in his usual dramatic fashion.

'What do you mean?' I asked. I had a feeling I

knew where his mind was going, though.

'We're assuming it was suicide,' he said. I flinched. No one had actually said it was that yet, but that was the assumption.

'But what if it wasn't?' he continued. 'What if someone wanted to stop him becoming a gay role model? Maybe someone killed him to stop him from coming out.'

9

BREAKING NEWS: SHOCK DEATH OF KIERON JUNIPER

A body recovered at Beachy Head, East Sussex, last night is thought to be that of well-known footballer and celebrity, Beachy Head United captain Kieron Juniper.

The body was discovered at around 11pm last night. A vehicle was also thought to be at the foot of the famous cliffs, but is still being recovered by the Coastguard Search & Rescue team.

Kieron, 25, is survived by girlfriend Ellie Marsden, 24, also well known in celebrity circles. The pair were at a private function at nearby Beachy Head Stadium, the home of Kieron's football club. It is rumoured that an incident occurred at this function but this newspaper is not making further comment until this is confirmed.

Beachy Head FC were not available for comment at this time.

The death is not thought to be suspicious, but we are still awaiting confirmation from Sussex Police.

Comments

What a shock. RIP Kieron.

'Not thought to be suspicious'... 'incident at the club'... I hope this isn't what I think it is.

A player of a generation. RIP.

No, this can't be real. Not Kieron Juniper. RIP.

A young life gone. These rich young footballers, they get too much too soon. It's too much for them to cope with.

Chloe and Danny were best friends with Kieron and Ellie. Poor Chloe, hope she is okay xoxo

There'll be a lot more to this. You watch.

10

I woke up much later than normal the following morning: nearly 11am. At least it was a Saturday. We'd had a late night discussing Kieron's death, and I'd then spent much of the night awake thinking about what Noah said.

It's very easy to take Noah's ideas with a pinch of salt; he is obsessed with murder mysteries and sees potential cases everywhere we go. But he had been correct the two previous times he's said this, so it was possible that he was correct again.

And I was struggling with the idea that Kieron had taken his life. When we saw him, he was upset, conflicted, confused. But I saw nothing to suggest that he was suicidal, though I'd obviously only met him once and briefly.

I just couldn't get Noah's words out of my head. *Maybe someone killed him to stop him from coming out.* But who would want to prevent it so much that they would murder him?

The club and his agent were doing their best to keep it quiet beforehand, taking Fiona's phone and threatening legal action. But that wasn't tantamount to planning murder. Although Patrick had emphasised the enormity of the revelation, saying that it would change everything forever for Kieron, the club and English football. Wasn't that enough to kill for if someone didn't want that to happen?

And how could it even be murder? Kieron had driven off in his car, alone, and either accidentally or intentionally, his car had been driven off the cliff. Unless...

DC Wood picked up the phone almost straightaway, as I sat up straighter in bed to speak to him. I asked him what I wanted to know.

'Forensics on the car? Yeah, they'll do them as matter as routine, I think, but I'll check with Appleby. We're not treating it as suspicious though, unless anything changes.'

I asked him my next question.

'Jesus, Edward! Is that what you think happened?'

'Not necessarily. It just occurred to me it could have,' I explained. I didn't give him any other context or tell him about the revelation before Kieron died. Not yet.

'I'm pretty sure they'd check for that anyway, but I'll give them a ring and make sure they do,' he said.

'Thanks, Dean, I appreciate it.' I had a feeling he'd help me. DC Wood had been promoted on the strength of his work with me on the snow day case, and he'd remained grateful since. Not to mention, people in our village show a loyalty to each other.

'I was going to call you anyway, but it was too late last night by the time we finished,' he said. 'I've got something for you. Don't let on I've told you anything though, Appleby will be after my head on a plate.'

I rolled my eyes. Appleby had bent the rules enough himself in that regard; he'd even had me dealing with a case on his behalf when the snowstorm stopped him from accessing the village. 'Of course, go on.'

'We found something on the grass bank just before the cliff edge. It looks like he threw his phone out of the car before it went over.'

'What? Why would he do that?' I wondered out loud.

'I was hoping you could tell me,' Wood replied. 'Didn't you mention something last night about an important note on there, that the girlfriend saw? Could it be a suicide note?'

No, not a suicide note. Of course, I heard Ellie say she'd seen a draft message in Notes about coming out.

I explained briefly to Wood (without going into detail about the coming out) and he promised to let me know as soon as he heard anything about what was on the phone, as well as the results of forensics on the car.

Maybe he'd thrown the phone out of the window to make sure his coming out story still got heard. But if he wanted that, what was the reason for plummeting to his death?

The thought entered my head again. Maybe he didn't choose to. Maybe someone really didn't want that coming out message being seen.

11

My original plan for that Saturday was to spend the day reading. I'd received a delivery of some lovely antique editions of Miss Marple novels and I had my weekend planned around re-reading *Murder at the Vicarage*, *The Body in the Library* et al.

Instead, I'd spent the last two hours on my laptop at the kitchen table, reading up on Kieron Juniper and the general antics of the Beachy Head United team. Juniper himself seemed well behaved; most news stories I found were about his success on the pitch or his successful relationship with Ellie.

They were very much the media dream couple: childhood sweethearts in Brighton long before Kieron's fame, they'd entered the spotlight together and seemed happy in it. They'd got engaged last year, and although they'd announced a long engagement, the press were having a field day speculating on the wedding. No public rows, no scandals, no affairs or one-night stands, and certainly nothing to suggest Kieron was secretly gay. To the public eye, they were a happy and much loved young couple.

Similarly, Kieron's football career seemed exemplary. Signed with Beachy Head United from a young age, he was credited for the team's rise through the football ranks to the Premier League: first with his fantastic goal scoring form, and later with his leadership and influence as team captain.

He also had many caps playing for England, won several 'player of the year' awards and been the subject of bidding wars between all the big teams, but always stayed loyal to his home club. Then there was his charity and community work, most famously leading a campaign to provide more computers for schools. I found so many quotes from players, celebrities and even MPs praising him; no one had a bad word to say.

The same couldn't be said for some of the other players in the team. As I'd guessed, Ricky Roberts had a colourful history which involved scraps on and off the pitch, several kiss and tells and unsuccessful flings with numerous reality TV 'stars' from Love Island and similar shows. One of these young women had also accused him of sharing inappropriate pictures of her after their split.

Even Danny Higgins had a mixed reputation in the media, despite his friendship with Kieron and relationship with Chloe. He appeared to have a 'party boy' name for himself, with lots of sightings of him in the usual trendy nightspots, often with girls who weren't Chloe. His most recent scandal was being caught attending a house party during national lockdown. There had also been rumours of several rows and splits between Danny and Chloe over his wild ways, but nothing had been proven and the couple always closed ranks and stuck to the same story under the spotlight. In fact, they too had recently got engaged and were planning a big wedding later this year.

I'd just started reading an article about the rumours of a gay player on the team, when I heard a knock at the door. Patrick and Becky had gone out, and I wasn't expecting anyone.

One thing I've learned though, is that you should always expect Noah.

'Good afternoon, Edward! We have a lot of work to do!' he said cheerfully, without waiting to be asked in.

It was only after he strolled past me that I saw he wasn't alone; Fiona was standing on my doorstep with an apologetic smile on her face. 'He has a bit of a bee in his bonnet after last night.'

'That's Noah for you,' I said as I gestured for her to come in. I noticed she had another vintage outfit on, very similar to yesterday's but following a green and yellow colour scheme and a bit more relaxed for daytime wear. I felt a pang of nerves when she walked past me, but didn't know why or what that was.

I followed her back into the kitchen to find Noah already sitting at the table and about to commandeer my laptop for his own purposes.

'I wrote that article,' Fiona said proudly as she spotted it on the screen. 'Although I had no idea it would end up being Kieron when I wrote it.'

'That part of the story's not got out yet then?' I asked her as she took a seat. I tried not to look too suspicious of her, but I'm not sure I managed it. I'd seen a few articles reporting his death, but nothing on Ellie's bombshell yet, though I thought it would only be a matter of time.

'No one knows about it yet apart from me,' she replied. 'And it doesn't look like anyone from the team's leaked it. Jackie Luton will have all their mouths clamped shut. How's Beaumont?'

I was thrown by the question, and it must have shown.

I'm not writing a story on him,' she added huffily. 'I just wondered how he was. Last night was meant to be his big night.'

'He was quite upset when we got back here,' I said.

'Especially when I told him that another gay player had committed suicide,' Noah added. 'But we think Kieron's death is murder now, so maybe he'll be happier about it.'

'*We* don't think it's murder, Noah,' Fiona corrected him. '*You* think it's murder. I think your theory is ridiculous. Isn't it, Edward?'

I didn't reply.

'You must be joking, not you as well!' she said. 'You've been spending too much time with your foster brother.'

'Yes!' Noah called out with a fist pump. 'Are we

going to solve another murder together, Edward?'

I had been wondering if there was more to the case than met the eye, but I also wanted to manage Noah's expectations. 'We don't know anything yet. And if it turns out to be something suspicious, let's leave it to the police.'

'You always say that,' he replied, while engrossed with the laptop screen.

'Come on, guys! It's not going to be anything suspicious. It's a clear cut story to me. Ellie found out Kieron's secret, told everyone, he wasn't ready for everyone to know and couldn't cope, got in his car and drove straight off the cliffs that just happen to be down the road from the stadium.'

I looked at Fiona in shock. At least Noah didn't mean to be blunt.

'What?' she said on seeing my face. 'Okay, it's a clear cut story, but obviously it's a sad one too.'

'Have you heard how Ellie is?' I asked. I hadn't seen anything of her after her bombshell announcement; she'd probably left the party early. I just hoped she had someone with her when she heard about her fiancé's death.

'No, I've called and texted Chloe a couple of times, but no answer. Though Jackie will have the WAGs on lockdown as much as the players.' She paused and looked at me. 'You don't really think someone did this to him, do you? How would that even be possible? He was on his own in that car.'

I was debating whether to explain the crazy theory I had about what might have happened when my phone rang.

I saw the name and excused myself into the hall, not wanting Fiona to hear until I knew what it was about. I took a breath and accepted the call.

'Edward Crisp, bloody hell, you've done it again. How do you always manage to be the last one to see them alive?' The voice at the other end blared out of the phone, making me jump a little.

'Hello, Appleby.'

'So, you just cut me out and go straight to DC Wood these days, do you?'

I knew he'd say this the next time I spoke to him. DI Appleby and I had an interesting relationship. Formerly my school bully, Appleby had been the SIO on the cases I'd helped with so far. Yes, he'd got to be a detective while I'd spent years reading about it.

But now we'd formed some sort of... what? Partnership? No. Alliance? Still no. An understanding, I guess you might say? Yes, we'd formed an understanding. Appleby feigned annoyance that I kept stumbling across his murder cases, but I liked to think that he didn't mind, really. Though I wasn't sure at the minute.

'If you have any information about a case, or want any information, you bloody well ask me. Then I'll tell you to mind your own business and leave it to the police.'

Wow, I'd really upset him dealing with Wood first. 'Come on, Appleby, I saw Wood at the scene, you know that. And I knew you were too senior to deal with the trivial things coming from me.'

'Nice try attempting to boost my ego,' he said with a half laugh down the phone. 'And how come you're so involved, anyway? How do all these murders keep happening around you, everywhere you go? Enough of this Jessica Fletcher crap.'

I ignored the insult, picking up on one word in particular. 'You said *murders*.'

'Yeah, so?'

'As if this one counted amongst them. Was Kieron murdered?'

I heard a deep sigh on the other end of the phone before he answered. 'I don't know how you bloody do it, mate. But yeah, the thing you asked Wood to check has come through.'

I felt my heart racing. It was a possibility that occurred to me, but I didn't actually expect it to come through. 'No, you mean…'

'Yeah, you were right,' he said, cutting me off. 'The brakes on Juniper's car have been cut. It looks like someone wanted him dead after all.'

12

'I'm hoping this will be a straightforward case, to be honest, mate. Forensics and CCTV should sort it soon enough.'

I tried to process things as quickly as Appleby was speaking. So, this was 'a case' now. But it certainly wasn't a straightforward one. Even if the culprit was quickly identified, there was nothing straightforward about *why* Kieron Juniper had been killed. It definitely felt like someone didn't want him to be gay.

I took a breath and told Appleby everything I knew, including the forced coming out at the hands of Ellie.

'Wow, Juniper a fairy, who'd ever have thought of it.'

I couldn't believe my ears. 'I'm sorry, what did you just say?'

The usually never lost for words Appleby spluttered in embarrassment down the phone. 'Oh yeah, your brother. Sorry, mate.'

No, it's not just because my brother's gay, I wanted to say, it's because that's a stupid, hateful, homophobic name and you shouldn't be using it, not least as a so-called professional senior police officer about a murder victim. What kind of idiot are you?

But I simply said, 'yes, don't worry.'

Appleby continued. 'Anyway, like I said, this will be a straightforward one. I reckon either CCTV or forensics will show that it's a case of the woman scorned.'

'You think it's Ellie?'

'Who else, mate? Whether or not what she said is true, or maybe her and her mate cooked it up between them, either way she hates him. That much is obvious. And no one saw her after that. I bet she cut his brakes and got the hell out of there.'

I shook my head at the experienced detective going for the most obvious solution. I knew what he'd say if I questioned it: 'some suspects are obvious for a reason, mate.' But that wasn't the part that stood out for me.

'You said "whether or not it's true." You know that in her outburst she referred to a draft coming out statement on his phone, that she claimed to have seen?'

'For God's sake, am I the last to bloody find out everything?' he shouted down the phone. 'Right, so I need to chase up CSI team again about what was on that phone. I've already asked them to hurry up with it.'

'Yes, surely that's the reason he threw it out of the window,' I continued. 'When I thought it was suicide, I thought it was to make sure the world knew about his coming out. It still might be, but what if he also did it to help us catch the killer?'

'I dunno, mate, he would only have a few seconds to throw that phone once he realised what was happening.'

'And yet he still threw it,' I countered.

'Why do I feel like this isn't going to be the straightforward case I hoped?' he barked. 'It never bloody is with you around. I don't know why I even entertain your ideas.'

Because I know what I'm talking about and you just think you do. 'The other thought I had,' I added, on a roll now, 'is Ellie said she saw the coming out statement but didn't say where. Let's remember that this news came from her best friend Chloe, who's engaged to Kieron's best friend, Danny Higgins. Maybe Kieron had sent it to Danny first and Ellie saw it that way.'

'It will still come up on the checks of his phone, then, and in our interviews with Danny and Chloe,' Appleby said decisively. 'Anyway, thanks for the information. One of my officers will come take your statement, and Patrick's, about your conversation with Kieron.'

I was being dismissed. Before I could stop myself, I replied. 'Wait, Appleby, there's more to this and you know it.'

I heard him scoff. 'You what?'

'Stop and think about it. One of the most famous footballers in the country is about to make history and come out, literally the first Premier League player ever to do it. And he *was* about to do it. He was talking to me and Patrick about "the biggest dilemma of his life." He was going to go through with it, we could tell. Then, suddenly, he just happens to have his brakes cut and go careering off a cliff? Boom. History prevented. And you think it's as simple as a crazy ex-girlfriend?'

I finished and came back to reality. Where had that come from? I'd been thinking a lot about what happened, about my brother, about Noah's research and Patrick's words on gay footballers. I just had a feeling there was more to it. But modern detective work wasn't done on feelings. And I wasn't a police officer. As I was about to be told.

'You've been spending way too much time with Noah,' Appleby replied before a pause. 'Look, mate, you know I like you so I'm gonna be nice about this. But who the hell do you think you are? I don't need you to tell me this is a high-profile case. I've had every rung of the ladder above me on my arse already. All the way up to the Chief Constable. Not to mention our Divisional Commander, with her stupid bloody Criminology Masters, reminding me it has to be evidence based.'

I could tell he was under a lot of pressure from senior police, and probably felt embarrassed to learn half the case details from me. 'You're right, I'm sorry.'

But he went on. 'No, Edward, it's happening too much now. Every major case I get, you pop up out of nowhere. You're an amateur, mate. This isn't a bloody Agatha Christie book, this is actual police work that we'll solve with evidence: forensics, fingerprints, CCTV. Not by the school librarian poncing about, thinking he's Poirot. Got it?'

He hung up the phone and left me to my inevitable anxiety attack.

13

I'd taken the call in the hallway, but stumbled my way through to the living room and closed the door, eventually finding the sofa beneath me as I focused on breathing. In, out. In, out.

As I did this, Appleby's harsh words stabbed through my thoughts, refusing to go away.

Who the hell do you think you are?

In, out.

You're an amateur.

In, out.

The school librarian poncing about, thinking he's Poirot.

In, out.

Concentrating on my breathing wasn't working, so I tried the 54321 technique that Doctor Albright recommended.

Five things you can see.

The sofa. My beloved book collection: I've got three separate complete Agatha Christie collections, so I cheated and counted them three times. I needed one more... my reflection in the TV screen; the image of the *amateur, the school librarian poncing about, thinking he's Poirot.* That didn't work.

Four things you can touch.

My books again. I immediately went to my

bookcase, knowing that handling my treasured Christie collections always made me feel better. I picked out four of my favourite titles one by one and studied the covers. I noticed the vintage artwork on one and spotted a familiar egg-shaped head: *the school librarian poncing about, thinking he's Poirot.*

Three things you can hear.

I fell back on the sofa and closed my eyes. Patrick and I lived in a terraced house on Chalk Gap Road, the main road on the way out of the village. Like most of Chalk Gap, it was a relatively quiet area, so I was listening for 30 seconds hearing no noise outside. But I heard noise from inside; I could hear Noah talking to Fiona in the kitchen.

'Now we know it's definitely murder, it's important to get a list of suspects.'

I opened the door to see an array of stationery: flip-chart paper, marker pens and post-it notes, the latter two in every colour imaginable. They must have raided Patrick's marking desk. Noah was crouched over the table, excitedly scribbling things down, while Fiona watched him.

'Noah, what do you mean, now you know it's definitely murder?'

He stopped writing and looked straight at me, unfazed. 'Oh, hi Edward. I heard your conversation with DI Appleby; we know the brakes were cut, and it's confirmed as murder now. So I set up our interview room.'

'Don't look at me,' Fiona said instantly. 'Though there's no harm in us speculating, is there?'

'You don't know what he's like. He won't let this go now,' I replied. 'And didn't you think this was ridiculous five minutes ago?'

'Oh yes, I did,' she said with a smile. 'And I still do. Which means this could be the biggest story of my career. It was already earth-shattering enough with the coming out, but now he was killed for it? Sign me up.'

I gave her the sharpest look I could muster and turned to Noah. 'And you. Listening in to my conversations behind my back, that's the respect we have for each other?'

He was still oblivious, despite my guilt trip. 'It wasn't behind your back, I've just told you.'

'Noah, I closed the door. I didn't want you to hear.'

'So I just listened harder,' he said, as he beamed.

'You obviously didn't listen to the end of the conversation,' I snapped back. My anxiety seemed to have turned into misplaced anger at Noah, and I regretted it later. But I continued, 'DI Appleby reminded me we are *amateurs*, Noah. He thinks they'll solve it with DNA and CCTV, anyway.'

'Oh, that's boring,' he said, unfazed.

'Yes, where's the fun in that?' Fiona added. 'I was quite looking forward to my first murder investigation.'

'And I've done all this work on the suspects now,' Noah said, standing aside to show off his handiwork with the flip-chart paper and post-it notes. 'Ta-dah!'

I stared at it, collecting my thoughts. It was difficult to stay angry when Noah was around. Fiona could see my resolve cracking.

'It won't hurt to have a look at what he's done, will it?' she said, coaxing me.

I took in Noah's giant, swirly red writing on the sheet in front of me. He'd written 'Kieron Juniper: suspects' in the middle of the paper, with various lines off leading to large post-it notes, each of which contained a suspect name and a couple of points about them.

Ellie Marsden. *Kieron's GF (ex-GF?) and obvious suspect. Obvious motive & opportunity (where did she go?)*

Ricky Roberts. *Motive: dislikes Kieron / jealousy? Could be homophobic? Other motives we don't know?*

Jackie Luton. *Didn't want scandal of Kieron coming out.*

Danny Higgins. *Kieron's best friend. Knew his secret already? Need to confirm. Other motive?*

Chloe Stone. *Told Ellie, so knew already? Need*

to confirm. Didn't like being caught out rumour spreading? Losing spotlight to Kieron?

Beaumont Albright. *Night ruined by Kieron's secret. Other motives?*

Fiona Turtle. *Wanted a major news story. Created her own?*

Other players / WAGs?

My first reaction was to laugh out loud at Fiona's inclusion when she was right there in the room with him, but luckily, she was laughing too.

'I told him to include everyone he thought of, no exceptions,' she said. 'Obviously I didn't cut his brakes, but keep me on there for now, it's hilarious.'

I glanced at the mind map again and had a nervous thought about what Kat would think if she popped over again and saw it. 'Let's take Beaumont off, though, shall we? I don't think he met Kieron before yesterday and his motive is a bit tenuous.'

I reached over to remove his name, but Fiona put her hand over mine and stopped me. 'Every name on there is a bit tenuous apart from Ellie, until we get more information. I think we should keep him on for now. That boy's so quiet: he definitely has something to hide.'

'It's turned out to be surprising suspects before,'

Noah said in a matter-of-fact way.

'Okay, fine,' I conceded. 'It's not like we're going to investigate anyway, let's leave it for the police. But Noah, will you do me a favour and keep that post-it in your pocket? He's Kat's family and I don't want to upset her if she calls round.'

He looked at me without blinking as he took the note away. 'Yes, no problem. But of course we're investigating, silly. Don't worry, you'll come round soon enough.'

'What is wrong with you?' Fiona asked in a raised voice, abruptly and suddenly. We stared at each other for a second. I took in the sight of her bright yellow, thick-rimmed retro glasses. Did she have a pair in every colour to match each outfit?

'Nothing's wrong with me,' I replied, before overcoming my anxiety to add, 'and that's a little rude of you to say, actually.'

She grinned broadly. Part of me was enjoying our back and forth, and I think part of her was too. 'Cry me a river, Edward. I've heard all about this anxiety stuff and I don't care for it, to be honest. Some two-bit copper calls you an amateur and you go crying away?'

'But, he's right, I am,' I started, but didn't get any further.

She adjusted her glasses, took her seat back at the table and spoke calmly, slowly and politely. 'Yes, he's right, you're an amateur. But an amateur who's solved three cases now, while DI Appleby is riding your coattails, pretending to the press that he did it all. He's embarrassed, Edward. And he doesn't want you poking your nose in 'cos he's worried we'll all find out you're better at his job than he is.'

I fell back in my chair and examined this whirlwind of a woman in front of me. She spoke a lot of sense. I supposed it would be fun to do some work with her; her capacity as a journalist would allow for her to do some unofficial digging around behind the scenes. And I felt drawn to her. But then I remembered Noah's inclusion of her on the suspect list. I tried to dismiss the thought, and I didn't think it held much weight, but it was a possibility still. I couldn't allow myself to become close to her if she was the killer. Not this time.

'You're right,' I said back, in as neutral a tone as I could manage. 'But I'll do my own thing. There's no harm in you looking into things with Noah, seeing as he's working alongside you, anyway.'

I saw the disappointment on her face as she glanced away from me. I noticed something in her expression I hadn't previously seen behind her tough exterior... what was it? Vulnerability?

I had little chance to think about it as I heard the front door go, before I heard Patrick's voice calling through. 'Edward, are you in? We need to speak to you.'

Becky's voice soon followed his. 'You'll never

believe who we saw on our walk this morning. Wait 'til you hear what we have to say.'

14

Patrick and Becky had fallen into couple territory quickly over the last few months, so usually spent their Saturday morning going for walks in our beautiful surroundings. Sometimes it would be the seafront, sometimes a trip to Brighton, or often a walk round many parts of the incredible South Downs which surrounded us.

This morning, no doubt thanks to Becky's nosiness, they'd stayed quite close to home and walked from the village over to Beachy Head. The main area of cliffs near where the incident had happened was still cordoned off (of course it was now a crime scene), but they'd got as far as they could before retreating over the road to The Beachy Head pub for a bite to eat. As they were leaving an hour later, they heard a voice from the corner of the pub.

'I couldn't believe that Chloe Stone was calling my name!' Becky said with excitement, star-struck once again.

Fiona looked surprised, sitting up suddenly. 'What? His best mate was murdered last night, possibly over a secret *they* let out, and they're off out having a pleasant lunch with a scenic view?'

'No, no, it wasn't like that at all,' Becky said, of course coming straight to her heroine's defence. 'They'd done the same thing as us actually, had a walk to see where it happened. Chloe thought it would help Danny. She's so thoughtful.'

Fiona's response was to roll her eyes.

'You should have seen him, buddy,' Patrick said as he took a seat at the table. 'He looked awful. He's in such a bad way.'

'It still makes little sense why they were out, right near the crime scene where all the press are going to be,' Fiona said again. She seemed to be firmly against the couple and their intentions.

'Actually, the press were hounding them outside their house, which is why they got out for a bit,' Becky argued.

'Fiona, didn't you say you went there yourself before you met me this morning?' Noah asked. Fiona went red and put her head down.

'You can never account for what people do when they're grieving,' I pointed out. It seemed like Chloe had her own intentions, likely linked to maximum publicity. But we were with Danny last night and I could see that his grief was real.

'You'll be able to see for yourself this evening when we meet them. I can't wait!' Becky announced with glee.

'What do you mean?' I asked.

'Chloe and Danny are going for a drink in Brighton to raise a glass to Kieron, and she told us to join them and bring who we want. Chloe's mate Troy knows somewhere just off St James's Street where the press won't find them.'

St James's Street was known as the popular LGBT area of Brighton, with its many gay bars, pubs and clubs. My brother and Dylan sometimes went out there, but not regularly ('we're not scene queens,' Dylan always says). It felt tasteless for Chloe and Danny to be going there to commemorate Kieron, not 24 hours after his murder; a murder that was potentially *because* he was gay.

Patrick could tell what I was thinking. 'I know, I've told Chloe it doesn't seem right.'

'Don't be silly! If Chloe Stone has given us the honour of an invitation to pay tribute, that's what we'll do. All of us. Edward, invite Alfie and Dylan. I'm sure they'll be up for coming. And Kat too. Fiona, you in?'

Never one to miss an exclusive, I knew her answer. 'Yes, I'll tag along. If Edward doesn't mind.'

'Of course not, that will be lovely,' I said, without stopping to think. She winked at me.

'Yes, you'll have to represent the Observer, seeing as I'm not allowed to go until I'm 18,' Noah said with a sad expression on his face.

'Don't worry, Noah, I've got lots of digging for you to do. That will keep you busy.' Noah's eyes lit up at Fiona's suggestion. I was impressed with how quickly she'd got a handle on him.

'Perfect, we have a plan!' Becky clapped her hands together in excitement. 'We'll meet at The

Chalk Inn about 7 o'clock. I'll book a minibus to take us to Brighton. Who have we got? Me and Patrick, Alfie and Dylan, Edward and Fiona. So, that's six for the minibus, seven if Kat comes. And we'll meet Chloe and Danny there.'

Patrick and I exchanged a smile at the way she included Danny and Chloe in our group of friends. Though I wasn't sure why she listed everyone in pairs as if me and Fiona were a couple. I wondered if Fiona had noticed it too.

'Oh, one more thing, Edward,' Patrick said to me as Becky engaged Fiona in some inane chat about what they would wear. 'This coming out note definitely exists.'

'How do you know?'

'Kieron apparently confided in Danny and sent it to him. I haven't seen it but he has it on his phone.'

Appleby had warned me to leave the investigation to him, and his words about me being an 'amateur' had stung. But, if I had the guts to, I had a chance to investigate further. I didn't have to wait for a forensics department to finish analysing the phone. I could find out that evening.

15

'Well Noah might not be over 18, but I certainly am.'

The first mistake I made that evening was allowing us to meet at the pub, where Mum had got wind of the Brighton night out and tagged along, taking Kat's place on the minibus, when she sent her apologies. I should have realised; there was no way Mum would miss a night out on the town with celebrities following the dramatic murder of one of their number.

The women chatted at the back of the minibus while I was sitting with Patrick, Alfie and Dylan. I wondered if there would be any awkwardness between Fiona and Alfie, because of her being his first and only girlfriend, but she greeted him like an old friend. I was actually looking forward to visiting the gay scene with my brother and his partner, although I wished for better circumstances.

'That conversation with my mum was the hardest thing I've ever had to do,' Dylan was saying.

We were discussing Kieron's decision to stay in the closet and his forced public coming out. Dylan himself had kept his sexuality hidden to his strict catholic mother, only telling her when he met Alfie last year. She had accepted him with open arms, of course, but I could see that the experience had still had a great impact on Dylan.

'Of course, it seems silly now that I didn't tell her for so long,' he said. 'But I was one of the lucky ones. Believe it or not, there are still some people who aren't accepting. I can't even imagine being as well known as Kieron Juniper and having to come out.'

'This is what I was saying earlier,' Patrick said. 'No one even knows how the football world would react, as there's pretty much no precedent for it. Certainly not in English Premiership football.'

'I think it would be alright, though,' Alfie said. 'Most of the blokes in the pub are football fans and they don't bat an eyelid at me being gay. I don't think they care as long as I'm serving their pints.'

'Just any of them dare to treat you any different and see what happens to them,' Mum shouted from the back of the minibus whilst still talking to Becky and Fiona. She somehow could be part of one conversation while not missing a single word of any other in her vicinity.

'Yeah, but imagine you were the top goal scorer for their team and you missed a goal, which cost them the game. Or worse, the goal scorer for the opposite team, who scored the deciding goal against you, which was offside. Some people in football crowds get lost in the excitement and sometimes civilised behaviour goes out of the window; they'll use any insult that comes into their heads before they've thought about it.'

'That's right, don't Brighton sometimes get homophobic chants from away fans?' my brother asked.

'Sadly, yes,' Patrick continued. 'Three Chelsea fans were kicked out of the Amex stadium on New Year's Day for homophobic and racist abuse. Thankfully, these kinds of people are the minority, but it's still an enormous problem.'

I thought of Beaumont Albright with his entire career ahead of him and hoped that being a black player wouldn't find him facing racism. I knew Kat was worried about that.

'But as despicable as racism is, there are lots of players of different races who all stick together to fight it. There are *no* openly gay players. Whoever put his head above the parapet might feel like he's on his own.'

'I think that definitely happened to Kieron,' I said. 'He described it to me and Patrick as *the biggest dilemma of his life*. It looks like he was on the verge of coming out soon anyway when Ellie outed him.'

'You don't really think someone plotted his murder to stop him from coming out?' Dylan said. 'It just seems so far-fetched.'

'Not at all.' I'd thought about this. 'You only need one murderer; it only takes one person evil enough or desperate enough to have the idea and carry it out. Whoever did this obviously had a lot to lose.'

'And whoever it is, this is going to be the biggest scandal in football in a long time. It's a miracle the media doesn't know it's murder yet, or about Kieron's coming out,' Patrick said before pausing. 'Or maybe not a miracle. From what we saw last night, I think Jackie Luton and the club will do anything to stop his coming out leaking.'

'Anything?' I wondered out loud. We hadn't given Kieron's agent or the club management much thought as suspects yet, but they were definitely worth considering. I hoped that Appleby's investigation would pick them up. Not that I would probably even get to hear about it.

Just then, I heard a buzz from my phone and looked to find a message from Kat.

Hi Ed, sorry again I couldn't make it. Went round to see Bev and Beaumont. We're really worried about him. Last night hit him hard. He's not sure this is the career for him. And neither are we, wish I could say more but I can't atm. Hope they find the killer – keep me posted xxx

I didn't know Beaumont well, but he'd always come across as a quiet, reserved young man who just loved playing sports. He'd been the shining star of all the various school sports teams as long as I could remember, taking us to many national football finals. For this to happen to one of his role models was heart-breaking. I also wondered what Kat's 'wish I could say more' might be.

I looked out of my window at the beautiful,

glimmering sea on my left. Tonight I would focus on finding out everything I could about Kieron's coming out statement, and hopefully even get to see it, as well as look out for anything that might make Danny or Chloe suspects.

Chloe seemed vacuous and publicity obsessed, but other than being Ellie's confidante, I couldn't see anything yet which would make her want to kill Kieron. And obviously we couldn't think about Ellie herself, who to Appleby was the prime suspect. I'd leave her to him for now while I explored avenues he might not.

As we arrived in central Brighton, I took in the busy, bright, late Spring Saturday evening. Couples walked along the promenade eating chips, families milled around outside Harvester and the Sealife Centre. Groups of all ages and numbers spilled out of the pier. This was life being lived, and it was barely twenty miles from our village. Why had I barely seen this sight in my 32 years?

The minibus turned off the seafront opposite the pier and we soon pulled into St James's Street. Again, there were revellers everywhere: students poured out of Sainsbury's and Morrisons with crates of beer, while hungry drinkers wolfed down Belgian chips in cones (I knew this because the shop was called Belgian Chips). I saw all-male groups that could have been any age from twenties to forties, walking along, probably to the next bar.

We turned off the main street, and the driver

pulled over outside a pleasant looking but fairly small bar in a red brick building.

'Everybody out!' Becky called cheerfully as Patrick leaned forward to pay the driver.

'It makes a pleasant change to be out with my glad-rags on,' Mum said, as she balanced herself out of the vehicle. 'Wish I'd worn more comfortable shoes though. I bet there are drag queens in here with smaller heels than me.'

'They look amazing, though,' I heard Fiona say. Fiona herself had gone for a pink version of her usual vintage look, though I noticed she looked a little more styled than normal: no cardigan or jacket over her retro dress, which also looked a bit more finished and fitted than what I'd seen her wear previously. 'But the only person who needs to be happy with what you're wearing is you, Mrs Crisp.'

'Oh, call me, Linda, my love. And I love your outfit too. You look beautiful. I love people who dress individually.'

Mum fawned over her some more while Fiona helped her out of the bus in her heels. I knew Mum wouldn't be able to resist winking at me as soon as I caught her eye; she's so predictable. The last thing I needed that evening was her on a match-making mission.

Once in the bar, I took in the purple velvet soft furnishing, unique art on the walls and mood lighting, though I'd barely adjusted to my surroundings when a piercing shriek from Becky made me jump.

'Ahh, Chloe! There she is! Chloe, Chloe, we're here!' Chloe smiled and beckoned us over.

'She's with a guy who's not Danny. Who is that?' I asked as we got near to the table.

'I wouldn't worry, love, there's no scandal there. Look at him, he's on the same bus as our Alfie.'

Yes, I remembered. Chloe's (presumably gay) friend had suggested this bar as somewhere they shouldn't be noticed. This must have been the man sitting with her.

'Hi everyone, thanks for coming! This is my absolutely fabulous friend, Troy.'

'Hi everyone!' He waved at everyone in a theatrical manner, and I looked at him for the first time. He had bleached blonde hair, designer stubble, an immaculate haircut, a distinctive orange tan, and a pierced nose.

Then I realised where I'd seen him before. This was the man Patrick and I saw leaving the VIP toilets, just before we were the last people to see Kieron Juniper alive.

16

'I don't get it, buddy. What does this mean?'

Patrick and I had excused ourselves from the group and gone to the bar to get drinks for everyone, politely ignoring Chloe's insistence on using table service.

We were trying to process what we'd found out: that the guy leaving the VIP toilets last night wasn't a reserve team player after all, but Chloe's gay friend, Troy.

Why was he there? And how did it relate to Kieron's murder?

'Firstly, it looks like we have a new suspect,' I started. 'Noah made a mind map of everyone there last night with a link to Kieron, and this guy wasn't included.'

'But what could his link to Kieron be?' Patrick asked needlessly. We were both thinking the same thing.

'I don't want to make any assumptions, but he clearly wasn't meant to be there. He wasn't with Chloe or Danny at any point, wasn't seen anywhere else, and had no other reason to be there. If Chloe had invited him, we'd have surely seen him at her side.'

'So, the likelihood is, he was there to see Kieron? I mean, to *see* him?' Patrick asked.

I thought about it for a moment. 'Either that, or

to cut his brakes.'

17

By the time we got back from the bar with our drinks, there were already several bottles of champagne delivered to the table, courtesy of Chloe.

'Enjoy your drinks, boys. You're missing my bubbles.' She gave us a triumphant smile which said *don't refuse my hospitality again.*

'Not many boys miss her bubbles, from what I've heard,' Mum said to me in barely a whisper as she drank the woman's champagne, which she used to toast her as she talked behind her back. 'Cheers, love, thank you for the fizz!'

'I can tell you a tale or two,' Fiona said to Mum in a low voice. She slid over to Mum as she said this, then poured them both a fresh glass of champagne.

'Oh yes, go on then, my love.'

Normally, I would stop Mum gossiping, especially within earshot of the subject. But, as a journalist, Fiona was as good a source as any on Chloe and there might be something useful: especially about her best friend, who might have been sleeping with or plotting to kill Kieron.

'Basically, Chloe and Danny don't quite have a relationship of convenience, but it's not too far off. She's always got guys sniffing round her, and there's quite a few girls who convincingly claim to have slept with him. There's more than a few compromising photos of him leaving nightclubs.'

'Ooh, is it one of those open relationship things?' Mum asked.

'I don't think so,' Fiona replied. 'From what I can tell, they both just turn a blind eye to each other's indiscretions. Either that or they don't mind the publicity of rumoured flings because it keeps them in the press. But they won't ever break up as they can make far more money being together.'

'No, no, no!' Becky said, leaning over. I didn't even know she was listening. 'Fiona, you know I think you're great. But they won't ever break up, because they're in love. Those rumoured flings are just that. And I hope you're not responsible for spreading them.'

Patrick must have sensed the rising tension as he stood up and grabbed Becky's hand to take her with him. 'Come on, baby, Chloe and Troy are on the dancefloor, shall we join them?'

Of course, Becky would not miss an invitation like that; she soon forgot the conversation and rushed off with him.

'I don't know why she's in so awe of that Chloe just because she's famous,' Mum said. 'She's nothing special. She pulls her pants down and uses the toilet just like the rest of us.'

This got a giggle from Fiona. 'I like you, Linda, you're brilliant.'

'And I like you, love,' Mum replied, before

looking in my direction. 'In fact, I was thinking, you and my Edward...'

'Mum, shall we dance?' Alfie said quickly, saving me from her as he grabbed one arm and Dylan grabbed the other.

'My son and his boyfriend taking me for a dance in a gay bar, that sounds fabulous. Let's go, boys,' Mum said joyfully as they whisked her away.

'Sorry about her,' I said, as Fiona moved up next to me.

'Don't worry, she's great. I love her gossipy side. She doesn't suffer fools,' she replied. 'And she loves you very much.'

I considered her for a moment. 'You're good at reading people, aren't you?'

She smiled, but shyly, and looked away for a second. 'I have to, in my job. I have to get to the truth of a good story.'

I thought about Kieron before he died, and how upset he was in the toilets. 'Even if the story is going to damage the person concerned?'

She looked hurt. 'Edward, I've told you. I could have published the truth about Kieron's secret by now and I haven't done. I haven't even leaked that it's a murder; that would be a career-making exclusive. All I'm interested in is helping you work out who did it. To get him justice.'

I felt the heaviness of guilt as my breath quickened, and I sensed anxiety rising. I didn't want to upset Fiona; I just had to be sure.

'What do you know about Chloe's friend, Troy?'

'Wow, that's a change of subject.' She seemed to relax again, my moment doubting her, hopefully forgotten.

'Not really. You said you want to get justice, that you like getting to the truth.'

She looked confused. 'What's that got to do with Troy Nicholson?'

'Ah, so you do know him.'

'Of course I know him. He's always hanging round Chloe, so he ends up in the gossip columns with her. Everyone knows him. Why the interest, though?'

This was the first breakthrough I'd had that no one else knew yet, and I was going to share it with her. 'Because Patrick and I saw him last night. He left the VIP toilets just before we saw Kieron in them. Apart from us, he was probably the last person to see him alive.'

The shock on her face was palpable; it was almost on the verge of excitement as I saw her realise that this was something big. 'Troy Nicholson was there last night? But he wasn't with Chloe at all; she's the only plausible reason he'd be there. Unless...'

'Exactly. Unless he had another reason.'

I could see her processing the revelation.

'Oh my god. Yes, that's it. I bet Troy was having

a fling with Kieron. He must be the mystery guy Troy was seeing.'

'What mystery guy?'

She poured us both a glass of Chloe's champagne as she spoke. I didn't tell her I hate the stuff. 'Apparently he's had a mystery boyfriend for a few months. A couple of mates who write for LGBT sites in Brighton have asked me if I know who it might be, 'cos they know I report a lot on the Beachy Head WAGS and he's always with them. But I didn't think it might be one of their boyfriends.'

'Is he a celebrity in Brighton, then?' I questioned.

'Oh no, only by association of the Beachy Head lot. He's a hairdresser; his barber shop cuts most of the team's hair. But he's made the most of his celebrity links to present himself as one on the gay scene. Paid PR appearances, getting freebies, own column in the LGBT magazines; they all go for it because they think it will lead them to the bigger prize of the Beachy Head WAGs.'

'Really?' The celebrity world, particularly the Z-list celebrity world, was one I knew little about.

'Look around, Edward. You see how few people are in here? And the ones who are, I've already seen Troy chatting with.' I followed her gaze to the only other two occupied tables in the bar. 'Remember Becky said Chloe's friend had organised where to go? He's got exclusive access to here tonight, guaranteeing Chloe's privacy is maintained. And with her status, and how much champagne she's buying, they would have snatched his hand off.'

'And you said he's Chloe's best friend?' I asked. 'As in a genuine friend from before her fame, not just a hanger on?'

'I believe so,' she replied. 'He's been hanging out with her as far as I can remember.'

'Can I ask you a question? About your career?' I didn't want to risk offending her again, but I was genuinely curious.

'Go on,' she said back with a grin. '*I'm* curious what you might ask me, Edward Crisp.'

I took a swig of the disgusting champagne for luck. 'It's just that, you seem so switched on and bright, and you're obviously a brilliant journalist.'

'But?' She let out a giggle again.

'Why are you so fascinated with all this WAG stuff? It just seems so shallow, and that's not you at all.' *You have more individuality and class than all of them put together*, I wanted to say, but I didn't.

'Thanks, I think there was a compliment in there. But you don't know me very well, to be fair.'

'I can see you have more about you than being a WAG spotter,' I said with a nervous laugh, taking in again her fantastic vintage look.

'Yes, I have lots of interests.' She ran a hand through her hair and played with the large flower in it. 'I love my vintage clothing, I love jazz music, I love reading. But not your crime fiction stuff, before you ask.'

'So what about the interest in celebrities, then? Is it just part of your job?'

'Yes, and no. The thing is, it's not *any* celebrities. It's this group in particular. I'm a massive Beachy Head United fan.'

'Really? I wasn't expecting you to say that.'

Her cheeks went a little red in embarrassment. 'I always have been. My dad brought me up to be. Way before the players were famous and when barely anyone had heard of the club. They used to play on a school pitch in Eastbourne, and I'd go all round East Sussex with Dad every Saturday watching their away games.'

'What made you so interested in the celebrity aspect of it?' I asked.

'Do you know it's only been about three years that anyone outside of hardcore fans had even heard of these guys? I just find it so fascinating. They went from nobodies to household names. Beachy Head United had the fastest rise to the Premier League in the history of football.'

I could feel the passion in her voice as she spoke. This is how I spoke about Agatha Christie. 'It's actually the players then, that you're interested in, rather than the WAGs?'

'If you're asking did you get me all wrong, yes you did.' She laughed again to show she wasn't serious. 'But it's their whole lives, which the WAGs are a big part of. Once the team was catapulted into fame, it was so interesting to see how it affected their relationships. You've got players like Ricky Roberts, who uses it to pull a different girl each weekend. And players like Danny, who get together with social media stars or reality stars to make as much money as possible together.'

She paused sadly, and I knew what she was about to say. 'Then players like Kieron Juniper, who didn't let it change him, and stayed with his same childhood sweetheart the whole time.'

She wiped a tear away from her eye. 'Or so I thought. Sorry, Edward, I don't know why I'm getting so upset. I feel sad, angry, guilty.'

I knew which one to address first. 'Why guilty?'

'I've always had so much respect for Kieron. He's one player who just *gets it*. He was never phased by their new fame, and he tried to use it for good. When Patrick was defending him last night straight after Ellie's microphone bombshell, that should have been me. And even then, before his death, I would never report on that story without his permission. I was just trying to wind up Jackie Luton.'

I wondered if that was true. I hoped it was. 'And obviously I know why you're sad, but why angry? That someone murdered him, or more than that?'

'Of course that someone murdered him. Like I said, I want to give him some justice.' I knew that wasn't all. 'I'm angry at him, though. If he was really gay, that's one thing. The situation's not great, but he could have spoken to Ellie and made her understand. But cheating on her, with Troy? That's not right. That's not the Kieron we all know.'

I thought about this. Even as a journalist, let alone a fan, did she really know these people from the glimpses she got? Patrick spoke highly of him too, but neither of them knew him personally.

'Do you think it might not be true about Troy, then?' I asked.

'I don't know, but we're going to find out. He's coming back to the table. And I'm going to ask him if he was sleeping with Kieron or not.'

18

'Hi there,' Troy said to us in a polite but clearly uninterested way, as he took a seat at the opposite end of our corner and paid immediate attention to his phone rather than us.

Fiona wasn't that easily defeated. 'We've met a couple of times before. I'm Fiona Turtle, the journalist.'

He looked up as if he resented it, paying attention to her for the first time. 'Oh yes, the vintage lady, I do know you. You write for that tiny village next to the football stadium, don't you?' It wasn't a question he seemed interested in getting an answer to.

'That's the one,' she said with a grin. I knew she was getting ready to play her trump card. I just wish it didn't involve me. 'And this is my friend, Edward. But he's just told me he's seen you before.'

'Oh yes?' He looked back at his phone; I could tell he wanted this conversation to be over so he could go back to posting on social media or whatever he was doing.

'Yes. He said he saw you last night, at the celebration at the stadium.'

Troy's head shot up. I could tell she'd knocked him for six. 'No, he must be mistaken. I wasn't there last night.'

She didn't take her eyes off him. 'No, it was

definitely you. I mean, you're quite distinct, and Edward doesn't make mistakes often. It *was* Troy you saw coming out of the VIP toilets, wasn't it, Edward?'

A year ago, I wouldn't have been able to deal with a situation like this; I've always hated confrontation. But I'd dealt with far worse than Troy in recent months. 'Yes, it was definitely you.'

He took a sip of champagne as he considered me. 'I told you, you're mistaken. I wasn't there.'

But Fiona wasn't done. 'Oh, it's okay. Edward's friend Patrick saw you too. He's over there dancing with everyone, but he should be able to clear it up.' She went through the whole pantomime of standing up to get him.

'Alright, alright, sit down,' he hissed at her. 'Yes, I was there, briefly. I just popped in to see Chloe and some of the other girls for an hour.'

'No, I don't think so. I was with Chloe, or in sight of her, for most of the night. I didn't see you with her at any point.'

'Look, what's this about?' I examined his demeanour as he spoke. It was a combination of anger, embarrassment and... sadness?

'I'll tell you what it's about,' Fiona started, but I nudged her to stop her. I had something to say instead.

'I'm sorry for your loss.'

'Sorry, what?' He definitely wasn't expecting

that.

'I'm sorry for your loss,' I repeated gently. 'If we're right about why you were there last night, this must be a terrible time for you. I can't even imagine. And I just wanted to say I'm really sorry.'

Troy looked like the world had crashed in on him. When he spoke, he sounded completely different from before. Emptier. 'You know nothing. Just leave it alone. Please.'

'Hi guys, what's going on here, exactly?'

I looked up to see Chloe back at the table, standing over us all with a big smile which didn't look too genuine. I wasn't sure what to do and hoped either Troy or Fiona would take the lead. Chloe and Troy were apparently best friends, but that didn't mean she knew about any relationship he might have with Kieron, especially as he'd been engaged to one of her other best friends.

The few seconds' silence felt like a few minutes. Was no one going to speak?

'Well?'

'Nothing, hun,' Troy said unconvincingly. 'Fiona was just trying to find out some gossip about one of my gay friends but I don't know anything.'

Chloe put her hands up on her hips and lifted her head high in a gesture of superiority. 'Oh, was she? You'd think after last night's tragedy, spreading gossip would be the last thing she'd be doing.'

But I'd quickly learned that Fiona wasn't one to stand down easily. 'That's not exactly what we were talking about, was it, Troy?'

He looked between the women, completely unsure of himself. I imagined it wasn't a position he was in often.

Chloe quickly ended the stalemate and took charge of the situation. 'I need a bit of fresh air I think. Troy, be a love and come with me.'

He made to stand up but didn't make it that far before we were interrupted again, this time by a shout from across the room.

'Chloe! Who are these prats on the door? They tried to stop me from coming in. Don't they know who I am?'

The person responsible for this cringeworthy line was Danny Higgins, who had at least two buttons undone on his shirt, and looked much the worse for wear as he staggered over.

Chloe looked mortified. Suddenly, Troy's run-in with us was the least of her worries. 'Baby, what are you doing? I thought you weren't coming.'

Danny was at least six feet tall and I remember the sense of him towering over us all despite wobbling as he spoke. 'What, and miss the special occasion? I mean, my best friend's dead, why not celebrate? That's what you're all doing, isn't it?'

Chloe moved closer to face him. 'Danny, either sit the hell down and stop embarrassing yourself, or get the hell out.'

Fiona raised her eyebrows at me, no doubt noting, as I was, the lack of empathy Chloe had for her grieving fiancé. Danny ignored her and grabbed one of the champagne bottles, swigging straight from it.

'To Kieron!' He shouted this so loud that the other tables and people on the dancefloor stared over. Chloe grabbed the bottle, and he pulled it away, trying to stop her. There was a struggle for a few seconds before the bottle fell to the floor with a smash.

'Now look what you've done, you idiot! You couldn't just keep it together, could you?' She gave him a little shove as she said those last two words. He instinctively pushed her back, and she fell into the seat behind her.

Troy jumped up and put his hand on Danny's shoulder to move him away. Danny was too quick for him and pushed him. But it was the words that went with it that stuck in my memory the most.

'Don't touch me, you bender!'

I didn't stop Mum when she marched back from the dancefloor and slapped him.

19

'What you said is completely unacceptable, buddy. Even if you're grieving for Kieron. Hell, even if you blame Troy for Kieron. Still completely unacceptable.'

Danny looked completely bewildered. 'What... how the hell do you know I blame Troy?'

'It doesn't take a genius to work out from the way you treated him,' Patrick snapped. 'We've worked out they were having an affair. And now we know you knew, too.'

'I didn't mean to call him that,' he mumbled back, almost to himself. I could smell the whisky on his breath, even with Patrick in between us.

Patrick and I had dragged Danny out of the bar as fast as we could. Despite his complaints and drunken threats, we'd walked him as far away as we could get him. The three of us were now sitting on the pebbled beach, each throwing stones towards the sea as the sun set above us. There was a bit of a chill in the air, and I shivered every so often.

'You know, it's probably because of language like you used, that Kieron stayed in the closet,' Patrick continued, as he threw the pebbles more forcefully. 'Small mindedness, bigoted. Is that what are you are, Danny? I didn't think you were, and I don't think any of your fans would either. You're not Ricky Roberts, surely that's not how you think? Is that what you think of your best mate? Because he went to his death at the bottom of that cliff because of views like that. You should be ashamed.'

'Patrick, come on, easy.' I'd rarely seen Patrick so angry in our thirteen years of friendship.

'I won't go easy, Edward. Why should I? The number of kids in lessons I've picked up for casual homophobia. *"This lesson is so gay," "stop tackling like a gay boy," "pass the ball, you poofter!"* I know you've heard it in the library before too. I love football, but so much needs to change in it. How can there be no openly gay players? I'll tell you how. Because of hateful rubbish like Danny spouted in there. Someone like Kieron as a role model could have helped change people's attitudes. But he's gone. And Danny gets to still be here saying homophobic crap like that. It stinks.' He got up and stormed away towards the sea, kicking pebbles under his feet as he went.

We'd already seen Danny's volatile reactions while drunk, so I was wary of how he might react to Patrick's speech. I was shocked to see him sobbing quietly, with his head on his knees. Patrick's departure had left a gap between us, and I felt too awkward to move up and fill it. I barely knew him and didn't really know what to do.

Why did every murder case result in someone crying in front of me? Noah's approach to our 'mysteries' sometimes makes me treat them as a puzzle to be solved, which in a way they are. But Danny's raw grief was a stark reminder that every single murder we'd encountered was much more than that.

'Patrick's just angry,' I offered.

'No, he's right. Why should I still be here? It shouldn't be him, it should be me.' He cried louder as my discomfort level increased. I could see Patrick's figure in front of me, throwing stones into the sea.

'Don't say that,' I said awkwardly.

'It should be. It's my fault he's dead.'

I understood that this was a common reaction when mourning, but when the deceased had been murdered, these comments could take on a different meaning.

I considered Danny as a suspect, and where he might fit into what had happened. I remembered Noah's notes about him from earlier that day.

Danny Higgins. Kieron's best friend. Knew his secret already? Need to confirm. Other motive?

He did indeed know Kieron's secret already. Ellie claimed to have found out from Chloe, and his reaction to Troy just now, disgusting homophobia aside, suggested that he knew about that too.

I could see his words about it being his fault weren't literal; I didn't think he had a motive to kill his best friend unless I was to unearth anything else. What I saw in front of me was someone devastated about his friend's death.

'It's not your fault.'

He lifted his head up and wiped his eyes with his sleeve. 'You don't think I'm the murderer, then?'

This threw me for a second. I wasn't sure who knew that this was now a murder case. He must have noticed the look on my face.

'Relax, it's not me. We had some cocky DI at our house for over two hours this afternoon taking our statements, that's how I know. Said his team was talking to everyone at the club in the next couple of days. It was in our group chat almost instantly, so all the club knows.' This topic had distracted him a little, and he'd stopped crying.

'The press and public don't know yet though?' I was almost certain that they didn't.

He laughed as he wiped his eyes again. 'Jackie Luton was straight on our case, don't you worry. The club is crapping themselves about what this is going to do to the club's reputation. But it won't take long. Everyone will know soon.'

'Like I said, it wasn't your fault. I know how people feel when someone close to them dies, or worse, is murdered. Everyone feels guilty.' As I grew more comfortable, I moved up into the gap Patrick had left behind.

'They haven't got as much to feel guilty about as I have.' His head went back to his knees, and I thought he might start crying again.

I put my hand on his shoulder as I spoke again. 'Haven't they? Look, Danny. Whoever killed Kieron, that's who is to blame. Not you, if you didn't do it. Which I don't think you did.'

He grinned. 'Thanks. But I don't mean that. Whatever the motive, it was of a direct result of Ellie outing him.'

'Which came from Chloe, and before that, I think I'm safe to assume: you.'

He nodded into his knees. 'Yes. It came from Chloe. From me and Chloe.'

I felt a shiver from the wind which was picking up. 'Yes, and if that led to Ellie's announcement, which led to Kieron's death, that's a chain of events. Don't you think every link in that chain feels guilty? Chloe. Ellie. Troy even. Everyone shows it in their own ways. You went out and got drunk. Chloe's hosting a champagne party. Ellie's disappeared off the face of the earth. Everyone feels guilty, and it's natural.'

'Yes, it is,' he replied, lifting his head to face me. 'Unless one of those people murdered him.'

He made a good point.

'I appreciate you being nice,' he continued, 'but there's a lot you don't know about me: the life I lead and the things I've done. Not everyone would think I'm a very nice person.'

Was this a murderer's confession? On the surface it sounded like it; someone like Mum would slap the handcuffs on him by now.

But no, I recognised this as more guilt. I recalled Patrick and Fiona's stories about him and Chloe, and the things he allegedly got up to: wild nights, other women, cheating, not to mention his homophobic outburst just now. Whereas Kieron had barely put a foot wrong. This was survivor's guilt.

'Danny, like I said, it's not your fault, unless you're the one who murdered him. It's that person and that person alone.'

He stared at the purple sky ahead of us as the sun continued to set. A couple of minutes passed where neither of us spoke. Throughout that time, I felt like he was about to say something, but he didn't. I saw Patrick turn and make his way back up the beach; I could immediately tell he was much calmer.

He went straight to Danny, crouching down on the pebbles in front of him. 'What you said, it was disgusting. Language like that makes people angry. Quite rightly.'

Danny hung his head and replied in a murmur. 'I know.'

'I know you do. And I know that's not you. That's no excuse though, you still said it. Whatever made you say that, no, whatever made you *think* like that, it's up to you to address that and deal with it.' Despite Danny's grief, Patrick wasn't making this easy. I wished he'd been the one to hear Appleby's similar remark earlier.

'I will.' I heard his phone vibrate in his pocket.

'But I shouldn't have kicked off at you, and I'm sorry for that. And me and Edward, we are both so sorry for Kieron's death. I can't even imagine what it must be like for you. Believe me, though, you won't have to worry about the murderer. Because even if the police can't work out who did it, I guarantee you, Edward Crisp will. You wouldn't believe the last couple of mysteries he's solved.'

Danny stared at me. 'Edward Crisp... I knew last night I knew you from somewhere. The amateur detective.'

'Well, erm... not formally,' I stuttered nervously. I was still uncomfortable when I was recognised like this. 'Murder just seems to follow me round.'

'You're not kidding,' Patrick said. 'You all should have run for the hills as soon as he arrived for that event last night.'

The two of them laughed, but I found the joke a little awkward under the circumstances. Danny's phone buzzed again in his pocket and he finally lifted it out to read his messages.

'Seriously though, buddy,' Patrick continued. 'If there is anything you can think of to help, Edward's the man to tell.'

'I told that DI Appleby guy a lot. I didn't like him though, and I don't think he liked me. He said he wanted to make sure he saw me personally.' I was still trying to work Danny out. Was he a good man? Probably overall. But I saw a fragile ego and low self-esteem despite his fame. I could see why he and Appleby would clash.

'I wouldn't worry. He had a warrant out for my arrest when our Head Teacher at school was murdered last year,' Patrick said with a laugh. That seemed surreal now. 'He knows nothing. But Edward does.'

As Patrick spoke, I realised something which amused me. 'Danny, you want to know something you and Appleby have in common? You both got a slap from my mum.'

The three of us laughed together, the tension broken. Danny seemed a little more relaxed when he next spoke. 'What do you want to know?'

I looked at his phone in his hands. This was my chance. 'This is probably an invasion of Kieron's privacy, but I only ask because there might be something in there that might help us. I promise if you say yes it won't go any further.'

Danny looked at me dubiously. 'Go on?'

'I think Kieron showed you his planned coming out statement that Ellie mentioned on the microphone. Can I read it?'

THE TIME IS NOW...

25 years is a long time to hide who you really are. A quarter of a century with a secret like a weight round your neck. But not for any longer.

I'm gay.

Being able to say those two words releases me from so much anxiety and upset. I can never explain how difficult it is to carry round this secret. Every day, every interaction, every relationship in my life is tainted by it.

And why have I put myself through this until now? Why have I hurt a woman I care about along the way? Surely the easiest thing in the world is to just be who I am.

The answer is football. Football has been my life for as long as I can remember, but it is a life which I always thought doesn't fit a gay man. As soon as you score that first goal, impress that first coach or walk into that first dressing room, there is an unspoken expectation to live your life a certain way. Being attracted to other men doesn't fit that expectation. Or so I thought.

It's taken me until now to realise that it doesn't matter. I'm me first, and a professional footballer second.

It's finally time to be who I was born to be.

The time is now...

21

WAS MURDERED FOOTBALLER GAY?

Premiership footballer Kieron Juniper is believed to have been murdered, Sussex Police suggested in a press conference this morning. The Beachy Head United star's vehicle was tampered with before he left a private function at the stadium on Friday evening.

An anonymous source has suggested that there was a public row at the event which revealed that Juniper, 25, engaged to Ellie Marsden, was really **GAY**.

It is understood that he was about to come out soon, but his fiancée found out first. If this is true, Kieron Juniper would have made history as the first ever Premier League footballer to be openly gay.

This of course brings in to question the motive for his murder; was this a homophobic attack?

If you have any information which might assist this enquiry, please contact Sussex Police on the number below.

Comments

Poor Kieron, what he must have gone through. RIP.

The poor girlfriend. That's who I feel sorry for.

The main issue here is that he was murdered. Why is this other rumour even being reported?

Chloe will be able to solve this I bet! Wagatha Christie! #WagathaChristie

Murdered for his sexuality in 2021. This story needs to be as big as George Floyd. We want justice.

Mistake there I'm sure. No way he's gay, too great a player.

What's that supposed to mean?

Exactly. Great footballers can't be gay?

LOL he's right not really. Name one. I'll wait lol

True hero on and off the pitch. We wouldn't have cared who you were. We still loved you.

Awful end for the man who made BH United what it is.

Are Danny and Chloe doing okay? Danny was close to him xoxo

Chloe on the case – Wagatha Christie!

#WagathaChristie

Stop trying to make that hashtag happen. It's not gonna work lol

It's already working hun! #WagathaChristie

Years after Fashanu, another coming out ending in tragedy.

Ricky Roberts wouldn't have played with him anyway. Look up 'Ricky Roberts 'no gayboy' on YouTube or TikTok.

He should have played for ARSEnal lol

Grow up, homophobe.

Dont wanna speak ill of dead but maybe its for the best. Dont think theres room for that in our sport

If that's how you feel, it's not your sport.

I'm a Brighton fan and we get so much homophobic abuse from away fans. Got to think he'd have got the same. Just look at some of the comments on here. At least he's been spared that.

Got what he deserved then... I'd have cut the brakes myself

Comments on this thread have been disabled.

****

MURDERED GAY FOOTBALLER LATEST: BEST MATE HIGGINS IN ALLEGED HOMOPHOBIC ABUSE SCANDAL

Beachy Head United player, Danny Higgins, best friend of murdered footballer Kieron Juniper, has found himself at the centre of a homophobic abuse scandal.

Higgins, 25, is alleged to have given homophobic verbal abuse to an openly gay man in a gay bar in Brighton last night. This paper has been informed of the language allegedly used but decided that it is not suitable to print.

This is especially bad timing after our previous report that Juniper had been outed as **GAY** on the night of his death. Higgins and Juniper were well known to be best friends.

Neither Higgins nor his fiancée Chloe Stone were available for comment. Higgins' agent Jackie Luton also refused to comment.

However, a fellow Beachy Head United player who wished to remain anonymous said: 'This is disgusting behaviour the day after we lost our beloved Kieron. Sadly, it doesn't surprise me. At least poor Juniper was spared seeing this side of his "best friend." At least I hope he was.'

Comments

OMG how could he!

Chill. Imagine what that guy's going through. We

don't know anything.

No excuse for homophobia. Ever.

Love that last quote, that's so Roberts lol

Haha definitely, I thought the same!

How dare someone come into our bars and abuse one of our own. I hope they fire him!

They won't. The Roberts homophobia video been out for nearly a year. They don't care.

They should have cared, maybe poor Kieron would still be alive!!

Disgracing Kieron's name like that, shame on him.

Did Danny really say it? Sounds like another case for WAGATHA CHRISTIE! #WagathaChristie

No wonder poor Kieron couldn't come out. With friends like that, who needs enemies?

Why is this even news? A player just died. That's the only story from BHU I want to read about.

Don't you think he might be the killer. Maybe he's proper homophobic and couldn't deal with a gay best mate / teammate.

So OTT. Don't be ridiculous.

Bet he's tracked down Juniper's boyfriend and sorted him out for Ellie LOL

Rumours are he said it to Troy Nicholson, Chloe's best friend. Bet it was just a personal disagreement.

> *No no no, you don't just get to be homophobic even in a personal disagreement, SORRY*

Poor Chloe, hope her and Troy are okay. If she forgives Danny we should too xoxo

What if Kieron was sleeping with Troy?

> *You've nailed it. Bet he was.*

What the hell is happening at that football club? All paid far too much. A disgrace to our country.

> *Don't include Kieron in that please. RIP.*

22

It took seven missed calls the next morning before Appleby finally answered.

'Oh, here we go. Look mate, I don't have to justify us in making a case public to you.'

These were his very first words on the call, not even a hello first. 'I haven't even said anything?'

'Seven missed calls, that says plenty.' Our last conversation yesterday was quite fraught, and this one didn't sound like it was about to go any better.

'Who even does a press conference at 8am in the morning?' I was shocked to have woken up to the news having broken. It seemed unusual for the police to have made the murder public anyway (everyone still thought it was an accident or suicide), particularly with the speculation circus that would accompany such a high-profile celebrity case.

'Want to keep them on their toes,' he said in a disinterested way, like he was explaining something to a small child he couldn't be bothered with. 'The public are going to go nuts now. The killer won't be able to cope with that kind of pressure. They'll slip up soon.'

'And was this your decision?' I asked. Yesterday, Appleby was frustrated that I'd been solving his most recent cases. He seemed to be pulling out all the stops to make sure he got this one himself.

'It was my suggestion, but the gaffer went for it. Like I said yesterday, there's a lot riding on this one.'

There was something else I wanted to know. 'And the leak about Kieron's coming out, is that anything to do with you?'

I heard a deep sigh down the other end of the phone. 'Listen, mate, I don't have to explain or justify myself to you. But I didn't, actually. His parents didn't seem to know anything about it when we visited, so it wasn't our place to. I'm not a monster.'

His poor parents. I couldn't even imagine. 'How were they?'

'Not great. I believe Ellie's with them now. Which works well for us, I want her where I can monitor her.'

He didn't seem to have changed his view of the case since yesterday. 'Is she still your number one suspect, then?'

'I can't say, mate. Though Danny Higgins is acting suspiciously too. But you might know more about that than me.'

Silence.

'I know you were at that night out last night. You can't resist getting involved, can you? Go on then, you might as well tell me what happened.'

I thought about this. There was more information that I could give him: the incident between Danny and Troy, the likely fling between Troy and Kieron. But most importantly, that Troy was there that fateful night and was a potential suspect they'd missed. I'd also now seen the coming out statement, but I'd given my word to Danny and they would likely have that by now anyway, from Kieron's phone.

I decided not to drop Danny in it further and told Appleby that I didn't see the Danny and Troy incident. I knew I had to tell him about Troy's presence on the night Kieron died, though; the police deserved to know that. But what was the harm in trying to find out what I could from Appleby's end in return?'

'I have actually learned something really important. Maybe we could update each other on what we know?'

I heard a loud guffaw through the phone. 'You're a bloody cheeky beggar, Edward Crisp, I'll give you that. You'll cost me my job one of these days. I've not got much, but there's no harm in telling you, I suppose. Go on, you first.'

I told him about seeing Troy and our theory about him and Kieron. 'How the hell has he avoided us knowing he was there? Lucky you saw him. You're always in the right place at the right time, aren't you?'

I couldn't tell if this was a compliment or another dig. I paced the living room, where I was taking the call, to keep calm. I looked towards my beloved bookshelves for comfort. It was important to make Appleby still feel in charge. 'What do you think, then? If anyone can find out if he was involved, it's you.'

'Yes, mate, leave him to me. It's an interesting one, though. He could be our killer. Maybe Juniper was going to come out, but he backed out. Troy turned up to try to persuade him, but obviously it's all kicked off with Ellie by that point, so that was a no go. Heartbroken and angry, he cuts his secret lover's brakes, sending him to his death.'

It was certainly a theory, and one that had briefly occurred to me too. But was it as simple as that? And what had happened to Ellie being his number one suspect? I realised something. 'No luck with the club CCTV then?'

'Don't get me started, mate. What kind of multi-billion pound football club has hardly any CCTV? Barely any in the car park or building. The footage we do have isn't worth anything.'

So much for his theory about solving it with CCTV. 'What do you have then?'

'Not much. We found brake fluid in Juniper's parking spot, but that just confirms what we know, really. Most interesting thing we got only turned up early evening yesterday. Brake cutters found dumped in the club recycling bins. And the club's tool cupboard was raided so we've got where it came from too. Again, it confirms what we know but the cutters are in for forensics, so I'm hoping they might tell us something.'

I doubted it would, but depending on how spur of the moment the crime was, there might be fingerprints on there. 'How did all the interviews go?'

'Sod all again, really. Ellie got a taxi home, which we've confirmed, but there's nothing to say she didn't cut her boyfriend's brakes on the way out. This is the problem, mate. Almost everyone was in other people's company all night, but no one can account for the five or ten minutes it would take to have slipped out. Could have been done while someone had gone to the loo or for a smoke.'

I was interested to know his views, though I didn't expect to agree with them. 'What do you think?'

'Not sure, mate, I'm thinking maybe Troy now. I'm going to take his statement as soon as I put the phone down. But I'm still not sure about Ellie, and I really didn't like Danny Higgins. Something about him I didn't like.'

Nothing to do with him being one of the star players and you being a Brighton fan, I thought to myself. We agreed to keep each other posted and were saying our goodbyes when he asked me one more thing. 'You're not up to anything though, are you, mate? That night out is one thing, but we don't need you and Noah going round carrying out your own investigations. We've got it covered.'

I promised him we weren't and walked back into

the kitchen, where I saw Noah had reinstalled his makeshift interview room. 'Okay Noah, let's make a plan.'

23

I'd felt bad that Noah couldn't come to Brighton last night, and I was more determined than ever to work out who was behind what happened to Kieron. This meant that I was back in a scenario becoming more and more familiar in the last year: the two of us working together to help solve a murder.

'The game's afoot!' he said with delight as a reference to one of his favourite detective duos, Holmes and Watson. This was probably the saying's most famous source, but I didn't tell Noah that Shakespeare used it first in Henry V. He didn't pay too much attention to any literature outside of crime fiction.

'Okay, so let me update you on what I've been doing,' he said brightly as he pushed my laptop across the table to me. 'This is the Ricky Roberts homophobia video, for reference.'

I pressed play. The video was pretty much as described in the article comments: a fan in a bar asked him how would he feel if a teammate came out as gay, and he replied no way would he ever play with a 'gayboy,' he would walk away from his contract first. He looked very drunk on the video, but there is no question of what he said and what he meant.

'Fiona's also contacted her mate at the newspaper who printed the Danny Higgins story,'

Noah went on. 'They wouldn't say anything officially, but off the record they confirmed it was Ricky Roberts who gave them the anonymous quote criticising Danny.'

I knew it would be, but it was good to get it confirmed. Did Roberts have any more to do with this than disliking Danny and Kieron, as well as being homophobic?

I began discussing this with Noah. 'I'm not sure homophobia is a strong enough motive.'

Why not?' he challenged. 'Most murderers kill to either gain something or prevent themselves from losing something.'

I knew his frame of reference was fictional killers rather than real life, but I understood his point. 'What would Roberts lose from Kieron coming out?'

Noah looked at me, confused. 'You just saw the video. He said he'd walk away from his contract. So he would lose his millionaire job and probably lose all the money he already has, in legal disputes with the club.'

I'd forgotten Noah's literal interpretation of everything. 'I don't think he meant it literally, Noah. He was just making the point he didn't want a gay player on the team.'

'Exactly. He *really* didn't want a gay player on the team. I'm not 18 yet and not of legal drinking age, but even I know people say what they really mean when they're drunk. And they carry out what they really mean, often ending in disastrous consequences.'

I was confused where he was going with this. 'What do you mean?'

'If he'd say something as awful as that when drunk, it could also mean that he'd do something awful, like cut Kieron's brakes. I estimated that when he was on the microphone, he'd already had about five pints of beer.'

'How do you know that?'

'I counted three empty glasses on his table, but everyone was mingling before that, so my guess is he probably had two before that, too. And his behaviour seemed to correspond with an athletic man in his mid-twenties who had consumed five pints of beers.'

I was stunned. 'Sorry, what?'

'Oh, I've been studying it. There are lots of YouTube videos on things like that,' he said as if this was completely normal. 'I'm 18 in a few months and I want to be prepared for when I go out drinking and what type of people I might encounter. Plus, I've been living above a pub for a while now and it doesn't do any harm to know how the customers might behave. Your mum already said I can do some shifts once I'm 18.'

I wasn't sure which image was the strangest: Noah on a night out or Noah behind a bar.

'Anyway, let's stick to the case, if you don't mind, Edward. We have lots to get through.'

I rolled my eyes. Working with Fiona had seemed to make him adopt what I'm sure he thought was a no nonsense, businesslike manner.

'So, these five pints were before everyone learned Kieron's secret. Jackie Luton then sent him to the bar with Beaumont, where my educated guess is he had several whiskeys and several shots.'

I didn't even ask how he knew it this time. I just looked at him dumbfounded as he continued.

'People always drink spirits when they've had a shock, and according to the internet his favourite is whiskey. And everyone orders shots when they're sat at the bar, don't they? But Ricky Roberts would have had a lot to drink, and who knows how that affected his behaviour.'

Bizarre close analysis of alcohol intake aside, I liked his analytical way of thinking. 'What about the others?'

'Other than Roberts, I think we need to focus for now on Ellie Marsden and Jackie Luton, as well as anyone else in club management who might have a motive. You've spent plenty of time with Danny Higgins and Chloe Stone, who are still suspects I'd say, but let's put them further down the list. I would have said Troy Nicholson too, but as the police are interviewing him today, let's leave that with them.'

I hadn't told him that yet. 'How do you know that? DI Appleby's only just informed me of that a minute ago.'

'Oh, while you were out of the room, I had a phone call of my own. DC Wood is very helpful, isn't he?'

I allowed myself a laugh. Appleby was acting like he was breaking the Official Secrets Act by divulging the tiniest snippet, while one of his DCs was sharing away with Noah.

He continued. 'Then there's any other club staff or players who might have had a grudge or a motive, but there's nothing to suggest any of them so far. Including Beaumont, who I think we can set aside for now. And Fiona's helping with the investigation anyway, so we can keep our eye on her while we're with her.'

I'm sure Fiona would be delighted. I wondered how she felt about the story going public; I hadn't heard from her since last night. Someone else had, though.

'Regarding Jackie Luton, Fiona has booked us in to have a meeting with her at 2pm today. You could join us.' He'd spoken to Fiona already too? He really had been busy.

'How's she managed that?' I asked.

'Since the stories broke this morning, Fiona's offered to do some damage control. Jackie quickly said yes, but could only meet at 2pm as she's meeting with some individual players.'

'Yes, I bet she is.' Roberts and Danny both sprung to mind. 'But that sounds brilliant, well done, Noah.'

'I thought in the meantime we could try to pay a visit to Ellie Roberts. But we don't really have a link to her. Unless we ask Fiona?'

This was awkward. 'Ah sorry, Noah, I'm tagging along with Patrick soon, he's going visiting Kieron's parents. Ellie is apparently staying with them so I'm hoping to have a chat with her.'

He didn't pick up on what I meant. 'Ah, perfect! We can go see her with Patrick then. We might learn something from talking to Kieron's parents too.'

I had a dilemma. Him talking to Kieron's parents was exactly what I was afraid of. We'd had a couple of incidents in the past where Noah had accidentally been a little too honest and offended people. He can't help it, of course, but I knew it might not be the best idea to put him in front of two grieving parents who were mourning their murdered son.

I didn't realise til afterwards that around 30 seconds must have passed while I was thinking about this. Enough time for Noah to realise something was wrong and speak up.

'You don't want me to go, do you?' There was no particular tone in his voice to suggest he was upset, or indeed any other emotion: just the words expressed in a matter-of-fact way. He looked straight at me and waited for a response.

What was the right thing to say? 'It's not that I don't want you to go, Noah. Just that it must be such a tough time for his parents. I'm going along with Patrick but three of us might be a little much.'

He considered this for a moment. 'No, you think I'll say the wrong thing. And maybe I will. I'll try my best not to, though. Perhaps we can have a signal or something. What if you blink three times if I'm about to say something I shouldn't?'

I pictured Noah telling Kieron's parents how excited he was about their son's murder while I stood next to him, blinking away. 'Maybe not.'

'I know I'm not quite an adult, but me and you are a team. I already missed going with you last night, and I want to be there for this one. And, no offence, I do sometimes pick up on things you don't.'

I weighed everything up. Noah had brought his A-game this morning with all the facts he'd checked, people he'd spoken to and work he'd done. I realised now; he was trying to show me he could still be useful. Not to mention that he'd shown awareness of saying the wrong thing sometimes.

A lot had happened to Noah in the last twelve months: losing a mum while gaining a foster family, and then finally meeting his dad. Maybe I needed to give him more credit for maturing.

'Okay, Noah. I'll check with Patrick, and if he doesn't mind, you can come.'

'Oh, thank you, Edward! Maybe I can cheer them up by telling them about some of our other murders.'

Uh oh. 'Sorry, what do you mean?'

'Just some of the murder methods we've seen: poisoning, being hit with a shovel, being buried in the snow, being actually pushed off a cliff. Their son just had his car brakes cut. They're quite lucky, really.'

Maybe I spoke too soon.

24

Kieron's parents lived in a converted farmhouse near Lewes, about half an hour's drive from our village.

It was set back in its own grounds with an electric gate and gravelled path leading up to the house, but otherwise wasn't as extravagant as it could have been for the parents of a multi-millionaire famous footballer. Though it was certainly a step up from the two up-two down terraced house Patrick had described visiting when he was young.

We'd driven through crowds of journalists and onlookers waiting at the gates; a few of them had tried to follow us through but Patrick pressed the horn til they backed away. Noah had his hands over his ears the whole time.

I saw a garage next to the house which likely held any cars they had, but then I spotted it: parked across the driveway haphazardly was a white sports convertible with its roof down (Patrick told me the make of car but I have no clue now).

'Maybe Kieron and his dad had similar tastes in cars,' Noah said, as Patrick tried to park without blocking it in. It took me a second to realise what Noah meant: the car Kieron died in was the same car as this, except red.

Who was it, Ellie? No, she was apparently staying with them but this car was parked as if it had just been abandoned last minute. Not to mention the insensitivity of bringing the same model of car he went to his death in, and then parking it right in front of his parents' window. Surely Ellie wouldn't have done that, but we didn't have to wait long to find out who would.

'Hello, boys!' We were just getting out of the car to see Chloe Stone totter across the gravelled driveway. Giant sunglasses, red beret, big stupid iced coffee in a plastic cup: it was as if she was a walking Barbie doll who had selected 'Spring driving outfit' as her accessory pack.

She took her sunglasses off to stare us down. 'I didn't know you knew Kieron's parents. Or are you just out doing your Hardy Boys routine?'

'I know them. I'm a good friend of Kieron's brother,' Patrick said. 'We're paying our respects.'

'What about you?' Noah asked her, in complete innocence. If anyone else had asked her this, I'd have thought they were being facetious.

'Oh, I've just been to see Ellie. She needs her friends around her right now.' She paused and turned her attention to me. 'I know you're the amateur investigator guy. You're probably trying to work out what you can.'

The focus on me individually threw me for a second and I didn't know what to say. 'Yes, erm, I guess I am. I don't mean any harm, though.'

'Oh no, I don't mean that. I don't care what you

do,' she said dismissively. 'It's just... look, I don't like you poking your nose in our business, and our reputations are very important to me. We're a tight-knit group at BHU. Your journalist friend Fiona will tell you that. But, we all want justice for Kieron. And I guess that's more important than what gets out to the press.'

'I'm glad you think so,' Patrick said, looking unimpressed.

'The thing is, Ellie said,' she started.

'Hang on a second,' Noah said, interrupting her. He took his phone out of his pocket and went into voice memos, pressing record. 'I like to record in case there's anything interesting. You don't mind, do you?'

She rolled her eyes, but continued anyway. 'Ellie just mentioned something to me that may be important. You might want to talk to her about it.'

This could be interesting. 'Go on.'

'The thing is,' she started, before stopping and looking back towards the house. She moved closer to us and spoke in a conspiratorial whisper. 'She's not doing very well at all. I don't know if this is her guilt for spilling his secret, but she's convinced that's not the reason he was murdered. But she's not thinking straight at the moment, so I'm not too sure.'

Patrick was losing patience quicker than I was. 'Just tell Edward what you know.'

To be fair to her, she looked genuinely worried about what she was about to say. 'She just kept talking about how a few of the boys used to come to Kieron with their troubles off the pitch. Danny certainly did. She thinks maybe he knew too much.'

Noah could barely contain his delight at this new twist. 'Everyone thinks the murder was because of Kieron coming out, but what if it was because of something he knew that he shouldn't?'

She continued. 'He was Kieron's best friend, and I'm Ellie's. I still can't believe he's been murdered for any reason. And the timing, straight after what Ellie said, is very coincidental. But yes, I suppose it is possible that there was another reason.'

'We'll get to the bottom of it, don't worry,' Noah said.

'Thank you,' she said. 'Just go easy on Ellie, she's all over the place. And whatever she tells you, please make sure it doesn't end up in the press, courtesy of Fiona. Speaking of that lot, I better go face the mob again.'

And with that, she fixed her sunglasses on her face, got in her ridiculous convertible and drove off.

'Is that all she's bothered about, the press?' Patrick said with frustration in his voice. 'A man is dead. She's unbelievable.'

'Patrick,' we heard a voice say. We all turned to

see a tired looking middle-aged woman standing on the doorstep. She was well presented, but one look at her told me it was in appearance only.

'Elaine, I'm so, so sorry,' Patrick said in reply. Kieron's mother ran forward and fell into Patrick's arms, sobbing her heart out.

25

'Would you like me to help make some tea?' Noah asked Kieron's dad. Patrick had guided Elaine Juniper back into the house, and we were now sitting in their front room.

Noah caught my look of surprise. 'I've read that when someone is upset, you should make them a cup of tea.'

'That would be lovely, thank you,' Kieron's dad, Michael, replied politely. 'I'll show you.'

I heard Noah carry on speaking as they left the room. 'Does she take milk and sugar? I don't want to get her drink wrong, she's been through enough.'

Kieron's dad wasn't phased at all. 'No, don't worry. I know how she likes her drink. I'll make it with you.'

I immediately liked Michael Juniper. He had correctly identified Noah as someone who might say the wrong thing to his wife, but got him out of the way with a minimum of fuss.

I looked around the room, taking it in for the first time. Kieron was everywhere. On every wall they had photos, memorabilia, trophies, medals and other souvenirs from his successful career.

'You must be so proud of him, Elaine,' Patrick said. 'Anthony is.'

'I think there's a photo of you and Anthony here

somewhere. I found it the other week.' She went to the cabinet and returned a moment later with a picture of twelve-year-old Patrick and another boy.

'Look at the state of me,' Patrick said with a laugh.

'Take it,' Elaine replied. 'Give it to your mum and pass on my regards to her. Tell her to treasure it.'

She broke down in tears again as Patrick comforted her. 'So, Anthony's back tomorrow, isn't he? I spoke to him on video call yesterday.'

Elaine nodded through her tears. Patrick had told me that his old friend Anthony, Kieron's older brother, now lived in Australia and was on a flight back, arriving tomorrow morning.

'I just don't understand anything, Patrick. None of it makes sense. Why would anyone want to kill my boy? And this story about him being gay. It just makes little sense.'

Kieron's death itself was the most shocking news any parent could expect to hear, but Elaine Juniper also had to deal with the added bombshell of Kieron being gay, and this being a motive for his murder.

'I can't even imagine how difficult this must be for you, Elaine. But as long as you're up to it, any questions you can answer for Edward might help us catch who did it.'

She sat up straight with renewed resolve. 'Yes, of course. Michael and I both agreed Edward should come with you to see us.' She turned to me. 'Edward, we've heard so many positive things about you. And God knows, that DI yesterday was useless. Please, help find my son's killer. Anything you need to know, ask away.'

I started with the topic she'd already broached. 'He'd never discussed being gay with you before, or gave any sign?'

'None. They always say a mother knows, and I feel foolish because I didn't know. It never crossed my mind once. I mean, he's been with Ellie since they were teenagers.'

I wondered how the two women were getting on under the same roof, and what Ellie's current stance was on her fiancé's revelation. Her own family didn't live in the area, and she apparently decided the only place she wanted to be was with the Junipers. She was now 'having a little lie down' after Chloe's visit and would join us soon.

'If he could have told me, if he only could have told me,' Elaine continued, inconsolable. 'He didn't need to hide it, not from me. But Danny was his best friend, at least he had someone to tell.'

'Have you seen Danny since?' I asked.

'No, I haven't,' she said sadly. 'He's messaged Michael a few times, said he'd visit us soon. I thought he might have come along with his fiancée, but he must be grieving himself. She didn't stay long, anyway.'

There was something about the way she said that which made me press further. 'It was nice of Chloe to come and see Ellie, wasn't it?'

'Was it?' she replied, glancing at the door. 'I guess so. I don't know, there's just something about that girl. I noticed she was talking to you all outside just now, with one eye on the press at the gate. She's probably the reason there's so many of them.'

I didn't have the heart to tell her that her son was currently the biggest news story of them all.

Just then, the door opened and Michael Juniper slowly edged through, carrying a tray of tea and biscuits. Noah walked behind him, reading his phone and not helping.

'Noah, what are you doing?' I asked.

'I'm afraid the young man got a little distracted. He's quite excited.'

'Edward, you won't believe it! Look what's been confirmed in the press!'

He came running over and shoved his phone under my nose while Kieron's dad placed the tray down with a dubious look. 'Elaine, I think you better prepare yourself.'

I took Noah's phone and looked at the screen. Troy Nicholson had confessed in full to an affair with Kieron.

26

TROY NICHOLSON: KIERON WAS MY LOVER

Troy Nicholson, Chloe Stone's best friend, has come forward as Kieron Juniper's **SECRET LOVER**.

This comes after Juniper's death on Friday night, with the police suspecting that his brakes were deliberately cut.

Troy released the following brief statement to the press:

'I confirm I was in a secret relationship with Kieron Juniper at the time of his death. This was without the knowledge of his fiancée, Ellie Marsden. I would like to offer my sincere apologies to Ellie for the hurt I have caused.

I would also like to publicly state that I have no part in Kieron's murder. I am fully co-operating with Sussex Police about my presence at the private function for Beachy Head United on the night of Kieron's death.'

Comments

Comments have been disabled for this article.

27

'It could be a double bluff. Troy admits everything, including his presence on Friday night. The police think he is co-operating and just feels guilty about the affair. But really he knew he couldn't have Kieron, so he was there to send him to his death.'

'It's a good point, Noah. Remember, we only have Troy's word for it that he was still even in the relationship. It could have long since ended; maybe he was there that night to talk him round but failed.'

We were sitting in the Junipers' garden, waiting for Ellie to come and speak to us. Kieron's parents were still very upset about the Troy revelation, so Patrick had stayed with them.

The expansive garden was on a slope which led down to a fish pond, apple trees and greenhouse. Sitting at the top in the patio area, we had beautiful views all across the Downs.

'Hello, guys.' Ellie Marsden was in a fluffy pink hooded dressing gown and matching slippers. She had no make-up on and around her eyes was blotchy from crying.

'Thank you for having a chat with us,' I said. 'I know we haven't met before so I really appreciate it.'

She smiled weakly as she took a seat at the patio table. She was being polite, but I could see her eyes weren't smiling. 'That's okay. I agreed with Elaine and Michael that I would. We all know your reputation. We want you to find out who did this. That stupid DI probably still thinks I did.'

'Oh DI Appleby? Yes, we're much better than him.'

'You must be Noah,' she said. 'I've heard how brilliant you are.'

Our first impression of Ellie at the celebration hadn't been the best, with our only time seeing her being when she was on the microphone. There was something about her though, that seemed genuine. We needed to hear her side of this story.

Luckily (or maybe not), Noah was on hand to prompt her. 'Are you upset about Troy's story breaking in the press?'

She took a few moments before she answered. 'I don't even know what to think anymore. Surprised, upset, shocked, angry, heartbroken... they're all just merging into one at the moment.'

I could see and hear this mix of emotions in her face and voice, but she didn't seem like someone who'd just found this out by reading an article a few minutes ago. 'Chloe told you about it when she came round earlier, didn't she?'

She attempted to smile again. 'They're right about you being a good detective, then. Yes, she did. She got to the bottom of it after Danny kicked off at Troy last night. I believe you were there.

Anyway, Troy told her he wanted to go public. When she couldn't persuade him not to, she thought the least she could do was come and tell me first.'

The friendship between the two women seemed to still be intact. 'You don't blame her, then?'

'No, course I don't. She was the one who told me. I mean, I suppose you're saying that her telling me set off the entire chain of events that led to his death, but that's not Chloe's fault. I'll have to live with my part in that for the rest of my life.'

It was time to find out what happened between the two couples earlier that night. 'Can you tell me about it in your own words?'

'Hang on a second!' Noah said, before pressing record in his voice memos on his phone.

'Are you sure you don't mind?' I said.

'Not at all,' she replied. 'I trust him not to sell it to a newspaper or anything.'

'Of course not,' Noah said. 'I won't even give it to Fiona.'

She started her story. 'Kieron seemed off all day that day from when he came back from training, just like really agitated. We were getting a taxi to the function with Chloe and Danny. It was all arranged, but at the last minute he said he'd drive and pick them up.

'When those two got in the car, I could tell there was something going on with them all. The entire atmosphere was just really strange, like they all knew something I didn't. We arrived at the stadium and Chloe asked could she stay in the car with me a moment and speak to me. Then she told me. She got it out of Danny earlier that day and insisted on telling me, which led those two to argue. Then I think he must have tipped Kieron off that she knew, which was probably why he was so off.'

She filled in the couple of questions I had: that Chloe had got Kieron's statement from Danny and showed her, and that Kieron had admitted it to her himself.

'Did he actually admit it, though?' Noah asked.

'Pretty much,' she said. 'He just kept saying that it wasn't what I thought. It was much more complex, but we should wait and talk about it at home. He obviously meant the Troy stuff.'

There was something else I wanted to know: 'what made you come here, to his parents?'

'It just felt like the right place to be. I've been with Kieron since we were 16, they're like my second family. Whatever Kieron did, they've lost their son. I knew they'd understand like no one else would.'

'Chloe said that you think maybe the murder was nothing to do with Kieron being gay,' Noah said in his usual matter-of-fact way.

'I don't.' She replied quickly, without even

hesitating.

'You don't even think it could be Troy?' he asked.

She took a little longer this time, flinching at the mention of his name. 'I suppose it could be, but I doubt it. I just keep thinking, what if someone wanted him dead and used this to get their chance?'

'When everyone will think it's because of him coming out!' Noah said in excitement. 'This is a classic murder mystery twist.'

She looked puzzled, but continued anyway. 'As captain, Kieron had quite a lot of players come to him for help and advice, so he would know a lot about his teammates that others didn't. Danny's mental health troubles, for example: him and Chloe have told you about it, I'm sure.'

They hadn't, but it made sense. Living a life in the spotlight was a tremendous pressure on anyone, and it seemed like they were constantly in it. Not to mention the rumours Fiona mentioned about the state of their relationship.

I thought about how he acted on the beach. I'd taken it as grief, as guilt, but looking back I could see how this could be a man struggling with depression.

Ellie had more revelations, though. 'But it wasn't just Danny. Kieron had been trying to help Ricky Roberts with his gambling problems.'

This was news indeed. 'Hang on, he doesn't even

like Kieron?'

She nodded. 'Exactly, he doesn't now. Note I said, *trying* to help. Roberts doesn't exactly want it. But Kieron could see it spiralling out of control and was trying to get him to seek support for it. He even involved Jackie Luton, as they both have her for an agent, but she just brushed it under the carpet. Was more worried about the story getting out.'

'So you think Roberts used the chance to get Kieron out of the way?'

She had a determination in her voice when she spoke. 'Yes. Apparently he threatened Kieron after training yesterday, too. Yes, I think Ricky Roberts killed my fiancé.'

'You two took your time, we're five minutes late. Jackie Luton hates people being late.'

We'd finished up with Ellie, and Patrick drove us back past Chalk Gap and dropped us off at Beachy Head Stadium, where Fiona was not quite patiently waiting for us in the car park, in a purple ensemble vintage outfit. I thought it may have still been closed off as a crime scene, but it seemed to be open again.

'I can't believe you went to see Ellie without me,' she complained as we walked. 'We're working together, Noah. Am I going to have to put tracking on your phone?'

'Sorry, we found out some interesting twists, though!' Noah replied, while I hoped she was joking about the tracker, as it wasn't a very honest journalistic technique.

'Yeah, Edward texted me about the Ricky Roberts gambling thing. But now there's the Troy revelation going public too,' she said with a hint of bitterness to her tone. 'Yet another world exclusive I've missed out on. The South Downs Star has got every single breaking story first. How are they doing it?'

'Yes, you said Jackie Luton won't allow anyone to speak to the press,' Noah chipped in, clearly loving his role in journalism.

'Troy Nicholson isn't represented by her and

has no affiliation with the club, and he wasn't disclosing anything that happened at the stadium,' I pointed out. 'She wouldn't have been able to stop him speaking to whoever he wanted.'

'She'd have expected Chloe or Danny to, though. Heads will roll for this.' I hoped Fiona was still speaking metaphorically. How far would Jackie go to keep her players' secrets quiet?

A few minutes later, I got a better impression by meeting the woman herself. Her office showed no sign of a partner or family, no photos, no trinkets, and every sign of a lonely, overworked singleton: several stained coffee cups and an overflowing bin with empty soft drink cans and takeaway wrappers.

'What can I do for you, Fiona?' Jackie snapped from behind her desk after Fiona had introduced me and Noah. 'Or more, what do you think you can do for me?'

'I know you're having a lot of the trouble with the press,' Fiona replied, sweetly and politely.

'And you think I'm going to make that even worse by talking to you? You must be joking.'

'Why did you agree to see me then?' Fiona asked in reply.

Jackie opened a can of Diet Coke within reach of her. 'I was intrigued.'

'You should be,' Fiona batted back. 'The last thing you need is hassle from the police too.'

'I'll give you that one,' Jackie said as she took a swig of her soft drink. 'They've been sniffing around for two days now, with their crime scenes and witness statements and court orders. I don't know what they think they're going to find.'

A man had died, and the obstructiveness of this woman considering this was too frustrating to stop me from speaking. 'Kieron's killer, of course.'

She moved her full attention to me. 'Well, well, well, it speaks.'

'I speak too!' Noah said, half waving his hand, completely missing her sarcasm.

She ignored him and carried on. 'Alright Fiona, what's going on? Why have you got the Rain Men with you?'

'You might know Edward as the guy who's helped the police in some murder cases in Chalk Gap,' Fiona said, gesturing to me.

'Ah yes, the inbred village you live in.' I did not like this woman.

'Quite rude, but anyway. Edward's become quite the expert in these matters and he's been conducting his own investigation independent of the police.' A bit of a trumped-up version of the truth, I thought. 'He might help you avoid having the police hang around much longer if you tell him what you know.'

She sat back in her swivel chair and spun the chair slightly from side to side as she thought about what Fiona said. 'I know him, actually. Edward Crisp. Anyone who keeps their eye on what's what needs to know who's in the local press. He's been quite the marvel.'

'Thank you,' I said, keen for her to address me directly rather than as if I wasn't there.

'I actually thought of offering to represent you if you got much more known. There are plenty of ways to make money from your Sherlock Holmes routine.'

I wasn't surprised to hear the 'money' word; I imagined that was her main motivation. 'No, thank you, Jackie.'

'I didn't say I was offering, just that I'd thought of offering,' she clarified abruptly.

'Do you mind if I ask something?' Noah said out of nowhere.

She looked dubiously at him and reluctantly nodded for him to speak. Usually I'd be afraid of what he might say, but it wouldn't be the worst thing in the world for him to offend this dreadful woman.

'I was just wondering, what your exact job is? You seem to be an agent for most of the club's players and many of their wives and girlfriends, which would surely be in the form of independent contracts between you and them. But you also seem to represent the club's interests too. For example, you have your own office here, which we're sitting in right now.'

She laughed out loud, before addressing Fiona, not Noah. 'This guy's a treat. I love him. He'd be great sitting in on some of my contract negotiations.'

Noah, as usual, missed the sarcasm. 'I'd love to, but I'm not an expert in contract law. I'm halfway through my A Level in Law though, I can check if it's coming up on the syllabus.'

She laughed again but replied to Noah directly this time. 'I was only joking, darling. But I think you've got a cracking career ahead of you, whatever you do.'

I was pleased to see her appeasing him, though this was probably only because she found him so amusing. 'To answer your excellent question, my main role is as an agent, but I also work for the club part-time as their PR Adviser.'

'Isn't that a conflict of interests?' Noah asked.

She scoffed. 'I don't care about things like that, sweetheart. Besides, I'm not there doing the donkey work, writing press releases and sending tweets. I'm there in a consultancy capacity. And getting paid handsomely for it too.'

I saw Fiona pull a face. The amount of money this woman likely made was probably obscene.

Finally, Jackie turned back to me. 'Go on how can we help each other?'

I took a breath. 'Talk me through the night as

you know it.'

She did. Her version offered nothing different from everyone else's version, but I wasn't expecting it to. It seemed like everyone linked to the club had the same story. That wasn't what interested me, though. I knew she'd give me an official, pre-agreed account. I was more keen to see what she was like, and what I could learn from what she wasn't saying.

'Who do you think killed Kieron, then?' I asked. 'It had to be someone there that night.'

'You were all there,' she said, raising her eyebrows. 'But from the likely suspects, my money's on Troy Nicholson. Spurned lover is a classic motive.'

'Oh yes, definitely!' Noah said, in delighted agreement.

I felt more cynical; I knew this would be her answer. Troy's story, for whatever reason he'd revealed it, made him the obvious scapegoat who wasn't directly contracted to either the club or Jackie herself.

'What about the club officials there that night?' Noah asked. 'Do you think any of them could have done it?'

'This guy is gold, he really is. I want to give him a job as my assistant, so he's around all the time,' she said through more laughter. She soon moved on quickly, before he could accept the joke offer. 'You realise that even if I thought that, I would never incriminate the club's officials, seeing as I work here. But, seeing as you ask so nicely, I'll let you into a secret.'

I noticed Fiona sit up with interest as Jackie leaned forward in a conspiratorial way. 'Those lot couldn't organise a piss-up in a brewery, let alone a murder. They're figureheads. They're there to worry about the football, I'm there to worry about anything else. Why do you think the club hires me?'

This felt like the most truthful thing she'd said in the whole meeting; I wondered if she meant she would actually carry out a murder if she needed to.

'Do you think it was true about Kieron?' I asked.

She didn't even blink. 'Of course it's true, his lover just came forward in the press, not to mention the coming out statement knocking about.'

'I'll rephrase then,' I said. 'Were you surprised by it?'

She smirked. 'You mean, did I know already? Let's just say I protect all my clients' interests and not much goes on without me knowing it.'

It was Noah who would step up to rattle her cage again. 'What if one client's interest conflicted with another?'

'Then I would act in the best interests of the club.' *And your own bank balance*, I thought to myself.

Fiona, who had said nothing for a while, spoke next. 'And what about some of the other things we're hearing? They could be possible motives. Like Danny Higgins and Ricky Roberts both having instances of homophobia. Or Ricky Roberts having a serious gambling issue, which Kieron tried to help him with and you allegedly stopped him.'

Jackie stood up and leaned forward, resting her hands on her desk. 'We're done here.'

But Fiona apparently wasn't. 'You're not going to answer me then?'

Jackie held her own. 'No, I'm not. It's a shame, because I didn't mind chatting with Edward and Noah. Once again, you manage to mess up, Miss Turtle. No wonder you're still stuck on the village rag.'

Fiona looked away, defeated. Jackie turned her attention back to me and Noah. 'My apologies, gentlemen, I do actually have a player coming in to see me, so I need to wrap things up, anyway.'

She took something from her desk and passed it to Noah. 'Here's my card. Call me in a year or so, when you finish college and let's have a chat.'

This move was probably to get one over on Fiona, seeing as Noah was currently working with her. But either way I hoped this wouldn't be a career option he'd pursue.

I had one more thing to ask her, but it wasn't

to do with the murder. 'This is a bit of a personal one, but I wanted to ask you something. Beaumont Albright.'

Jackie narrowed her eyes. 'Ah yes, his auntie is the Head Teacher from your school. The one Roberts was making all the embarrassing comments about. She's your friend I guess?'

'Yes. And she's worried about Beaumont. Even before this, it was a lot for an eighteen-year-old. But, now...' I left the sentence hanging as I tried to work out how to word it.

'Yes, of course,' she said, not waiting any longer. 'His big night was overshadowed. Don't worry, there'll be plenty more opportunities for him in the spotlight. He's going to be a star for this club.'

'You're really something else, Jackie,' Fiona snapped.

'What I actually meant was, it's the spotlight we're worried about. All your players and their issues they have, they all seem so unhappy.'

'Or they end up dead,' Noah added.

'Yes, I understand. Don't worry, we'll look after him.' But she sounded far less interested now. We said our goodbyes and left.

'I can't believe that woman,' Fiona fumed as we walked back across the car park.

'I thought she was quite nice,' Noah said obliviously.

'She's really not. It wouldn't surprise me if she

cut those brakes herself. I don't know why you're not suspecting her more, Edward.'

'I never said I wasn't.' It was my first time speaking to Jackie Luton, and I needed time to digest our meeting with her, as well as our conversations with Chloe, Ellie, and Mr and Mrs Juniper. I was sure there were several clues in what we'd heard today, that the answer was in there somewhere.

'Look who's there,' Noah said, breaking my chain of thought. Walking towards us was none other than Ricky Roberts.

'Hello, here's the misfits!' he quipped as he reached us. He was wearing a fitted T-Shirt and shorts (both designer brands but I couldn't tell you which) and a pair of sunglasses perched on top of his freshly cut hair. It looked like he didn't have a care in the world. 'Cracked the case yet?'

Fiona was in no mood for him. 'For heaven's sake, your teammate has died. Are any of you taking it seriously?'

He snapped back at her immediately. 'Of course I am. Look, I'm sick of everyone casting me as the bad guy in this. Yeah, I made a comment I'm not proud of. And I'll publicly apologise for that. No doubt Jackie's gonna tell me to do that anyway in a minute. But I'm aware a guy has died and I feel crap about it.'

'Is that because he was helping you with your gambling problems?' Fiona said.

Roberts looked like he was about to react in anger, but he never got to as we heard a screech of brakes. We looked over to see a police car pull up, along with another car behind it, which DI Appleby got out of. Two uniformed officers got out of the first car and ran over to us, grabbing Roberts.

'Ricky Roberts, you are under arrest on suspicion of the murder of Kieron Juniper. You do not have to say anything, but it may harm your defence if you do not mention when questioned something you later rely on in court. Anything you do say may be given in evidence.'

'Maybe he'll take it seriously now,' Noah said, as they put Roberts into the car.

29

'I told you good old-fashioned evidence would crack this case.'

'So that's why you arrested him. What did you find?'

The police car had taken Roberts away, but Appleby had stayed behind to have a word with me.

He looked conflicted about what to tell me, especially with Noah and Fiona next to me. 'I can't go into too much detail, but let's just say those wire cutters are going to be pretty damning evidence against him.'

'How did you know it was him, though? Have you taken full DNA samples of the entire team? Because that's really efficient police work if you have,' Noah said.

Appleby looked a little red-faced. Of course he hadn't. 'We started with finger printing actually, but we found a match, anyway.'

'Roberts had a driving offence when he was first signed with the club, years ago. You must have his full samples in your database from that.' Fiona really knew her history of this team.

Appleby looked impressed with her knowledge of the police. 'Fiona, isn't it? Maybe when I've finished with this case, me and you could go for a drink.'

'Oh no, that can't happen,' Noah said. 'Fiona and Edward clearly like each other. If she's going for a drink with anyone, it will be him.'

It took everything I had not to run away with embarrassment in that car park. I just tried to concentrate on Roberts' arrest.

'I see,' Appleby said with a grin as he went back to the car. 'I better go, I have a suspect to interview.'

'Will you let me know of any updates?' I asked.

'Maybe I will. But maybe you'll be too busy elsewhere.'

He drove away, leaving the three of us stood in the car park. I was glad that Fiona moved the topic straight back on to the arrest.

'There we have it, then. It was Ricky Roberts.'

'You really think it was?' Noah asked. I'd expected him to be ecstatic at the arrest drama, but he wasn't. He looked a little deflated. It was likely because we hadn't got to solve this one. I felt the same.

'You can't argue with DNA on the murder weapon,' Fiona said. 'I just can't believe it's one of the other players. This might sink the club.'

'Of course you can,' Noah said. 'People handle murder weapons for innocent reasons all the time in murder mysteries.'

'Yes, but not a pair of wire cutters stolen from the club's store cupboard,' she argued. 'What innocent reason could he have for handling them?

And this business about his gambling issues and Kieron wanting to help. If Kieron was threatening to expose him, that's quite a powerful motive.'

I thought about this. 'Yes, Noah, you were the one who said the real motive might be nothing to do with Kieron coming out, and the killer just seized the right time. Maybe Roberts did.'

'Hmm, maybe,' he said. But he seemed distracted.

'What are you thinking?' I asked gently.

'That this is a red herring. I don't think Roberts is the killer.'

It's often easy to dismiss Noah's various theories about actual crimes, due to most of these theories being based on books he's read. But I also didn't feel right about Roberts' arrest. It felt too simple.

I thought back to my feeling earlier that we'd heard some important clues today. I needed time to think about them, go over what we'd heard, and think about what it meant. I knew the answer was in there somewhere. I just didn't think it was Ricky Roberts.

30

Fiona dropped us off at the end of Chalk Gap high street to go to Mum and Dad's. I asked her not to drive to the pub, otherwise Mum would have surely invited her to join us for Sunday lunch. That would just be too embarrassing.

As we got out of the car and Fiona drove away, I noticed someone on the high street I needed to speak to.

'Just tell Mum I'm on the way, Noah, I just need to do something quickly.'

'Should I come with you? Does it involve the case?'

I told him it didn't, and he went ahead without me. I was half telling the truth; it didn't involve the murder directly, but it was someone who had been affected by it. I stood in front of the village square and waited for him to reach me.

'Beaumont!' I called out as he got within hearing distance. He looked nervous as he turned his head to see who it was. He would soon have people calling his name everywhere he went; I hoped he was ready for it.

'Sorry, Edward, I didn't see you. I'm just heading to the beach, to clear my head a bit.' He looked much older than his 18 years, with the weight of the world on his shoulders. 'Is it true they arrested Ricky Roberts? The team group chat is going off.'

That didn't take long at all; how did news always travel so fast round here? 'Yes, it's true.'

'Why would he do that?' In ten years of working at a school, I'd rarely seen a young person look so troubled. This was hitting him hard.

'I'll come along to the beach with you if you don't mind and we can talk about it,' I said in reply. As we crossed the village square, I prayed Mum wasn't looking out of the window, trying to hunt me down for Sunday lunch.

We both took a seat on the pebbled beach, a couple of metres apart. I had a flashback to my conversation with Danny Higgins on Brighton Beach last night.

'You were about to tell me why Roberts would kill Kieron,' Beaumont said in a low, quiet voice.

'He's only been arrested. We don't even know that he did it,' I reminded him, and myself. I'd been thinking it over since Noah said he thought Roberts didn't do it. I wasn't sure.

'The boys in the chat think he didn't do it. They're all saying he's a prat with a big mouth, but he can't be a murderer.'

'And what do you think?' I asked.

He looked straight ahead of us. 'Apparently Kieron knew some stuff about Roberts, and maybe that's why the police suspect him.'

I was pleased the bit about the wire cutters hadn't got out, at least.

'But what if it's something else?' he said. 'I heard what Roberts said straight after Ellie's revelation. I stood next to him. All the stuff about playing for the wrong side. And I saw the video. Where he said he won't play with a *gayboy*.'

'He said that when he was drunk,' I started, before realising I wasn't about to defend homophobic idiocy. 'Which is still disgusting. But it doesn't make him a killer.'

'Yeah, and he was probably even more drunk when he cut those brakes. He was with me at the bar knocking back shot after shot. And the police don't arrest people for no reason.'

'It has been known before,' I said, suppressing a laugh. But I knew what he meant. If Roberts was innocent, how was his DNA on those wire cutters?

'I've watched that YouTube video again and again. Yes, he was drunk, but there was so much hatred. It felt like he meant it, that he really would quit if someone on his team was gay.'

I could see that this was really playing on his mind. And I could understand why, having to deal with all of this at 18 while starting his own career. But this felt like something more than this.

I recalled Kat's text from last night: *'we're really worried about him. Last night hit him hard. He's not sure this is the career for him. And neither are we, wish I could say more but I can't atm.'*

Then I realised something. Patrick had

mentioned it briefly, but I hadn't dwelled on it. Homophobia wasn't the only potential hate problem in football: there was also racism.

I knew it had been a problem for years; I'd seen the news and Patrick had also told me many stories of racist incidents on the pitch. If the bigot minority could have a problem with sexuality, they could also have a problem with race.

'I know what you're worried about, Beaumont. I don't know what to say. I can't tell you it won't be a problem, because it might be. But the one difference I see between your case and Kieron's: lots of players are treading the same path as you, fighting the same fight. And the very vast majority of your peers will have your back. You can do this.'

He looked puzzled. 'Oh, you're talking about racism. I've dealt with that my entire life, I'm ready for that.'

Now it was my turn. 'Oh sorry, I don't understand then.'

He took a deep breath and spoke. 'Lots of players are treading the same path as me regarding my race. But there was only one player treading the same path as me. And someone murdered him for it.'

Beaumont Albright wasn't worried about racism. He was worried about being a gay footballer.

31

'I came out to my family nearly two years ago, a little after I'd finished all my GCSE exams. I didn't see it as a big deal, really. Not at first. I'd already told my best mates, and they thought it was cool. It was just a part of who I am, and is anyone really that fussed these days? That's what I thought, anyway.'

I felt for him and wished he could still have that perspective. 'But this has changed your mind.'

He scoffed. 'No, long before that. As my football career took shape, I noticed stuff. Comments on social media, the homophobic stuff that the Brighton team get sometimes. Then I did some research. The same stuff that Noah read off to us the night Kieron died, about the lack of openly gay players. I already knew it, but I know how matter of fact that kid is. I wanted to hear it in the worst light. But it was too much for me.'

I remembered how he left the room upset, and Kat went after him. 'Does Kat know?'

His face lit up. 'Yeah, she's amazing. She said I should make history. She still says it, despite everything with Kieron.'

That was Kat. She was always a fantastic person to have in your corner. Then I remembered her text again: 'he's not sure... and neither are we.'

If even Kat, who fought back against everything, was doubting whether he should carry on in football, it must be bad. 'Did you regret coming out then, once you saw things like that?'

'Yes, and no. I could never not be who I am. I've been out with one or two guys already and it feels like the most natural thing in the world. But it made me think about my career in football. When Beachy Head signed me, I just thought it will be okay. Cross that bridge later. But I wasn't expecting that bridge to be burned on my first official night with the club.'

'What about your mum?'

He released a big smile. 'Ah, Edward, she's been amazing, man. Always has been from the day I told her. She said she always knew and always loved me. It's her that makes me want to carry on and do this despite everything. I want to buy her a big house she can retire in.'

As he spoke, something clicked inside me. A thought I had, that if I was right, it changed everything we thought we knew about Kieron's murder.

I reprocessed everything I'd heard over the last two days, reframing certain comments in the light of my theory. I didn't even realise how long I'd been thinking in silence until Beaumont spoke.

'Edward, are you okay, man? You're miles away.'

I went to answer, but I was interrupted by my phone ringing. It was probably Mum telling me off about being late to Sunday lunch. But it wasn't. I saw the name on my phone: Appleby.

Did he have the same breakthrough I just did? I answered the phone to find out, nearly forgetting that Beaumont was with me.

'Edward, I need you to get to Eastbourne DGH as soon as you can. I need your help.'

'My help at the hospital? What's happened?

'Danny Higgins has taken an overdose. He's in a bad way.'

'Oh my god,' I heard Beaumont say next to me. I wasn't using the speaker phone, but Appleby didn't need it.

'I know why he's done it,' I blurted.

'Yeah, I thought you might. I know you were with him quite a while after that incident in Brighton last night. I want your account of what he said to you. It might help me if we get to interview him.'

'Interview him?' I ignored the ominous word *if*.

'Yes, mate. I mean, we've got Roberts so I don't know what's going on, but the paramedics said he just kept repeating the same thing over and over.'

I had a feeling I knew what it was.

'He kept saying *I killed him.*'

32

'I'll drive you. My car's parked outside Mum's surgery.'

Beaumont and I rushed through the square as I realised how difficult it was to keep up pace with a young footballer. We'd barely left the beach before I could feel a stitch starting.

We'd just reached Chalk Gap high street when I heard a voice shouting. 'Edward, wait, wait for me!'

I was glad of the excuse to stop running. 'Noah, what are you doing?'

'I was looking out of the window for you and I saw you both run past. It looked exciting.' He turned to Beaumont, who was a few steps in front of us. 'You're not the killer, are you?'

Beaumont didn't look impressed. 'Of course I'm not. Why would you say that?'

'You were running away, and it looked like Edward was chasing after you. I thought he might try to make a citizen's arrest.'

I explained to him what really happened as we carried on towards the car, and of course he wanted to come. 'I knew there was another twist to this, Ricky Roberts' arrest was far too simple. Let's find out the truth.'

'Why would Danny kill him?' Beaumont asked me as we got in the car.

'I don't know for sure yet,' I replied. I didn't. I

just hoped Danny pulled through, so there wasn't another life lost. And maybe then we could get his story, to finally get the truth.

'Linda's ringing me,' Noah announced from the back seat as we set off.

'Mum? Put her on speakerphone, I need to speak to her.'

He did so, and I heard her voice straightaway, not even waiting to say hello. 'Noah, what is going on? Why did you run out of the pub without saying? What about your Sunday dinner?'

'Hi Mum, it's me. I'm with Noah, you're on speaker phone. Just so you know, Beaumont Albright is with us, he can hear you.'

'Edward? Edward, now you listen here, I don't know what's going on but your dad works hard on this Sunday dinner every week. It's the one thing we ask of you every week, the one thing.' She paused, as if only just realising what I'd told her. 'Sorry, did you say Beaumont Albright?'

'Yes, Mum,' I replied.

'Hello, Mrs Crisp,' he said as he drove.

'Casper, Casper, they're with Beaumont Albright,' we heard her say to Dad in a failed attempt at a whisper, before continuing in a voice fit for the Queen. 'Hello Beaumont, my darling. I'm ever so sorry to disturb you. I was just checking my boys were okay and returning to our Sunday luncheon. If you are available, there will be a seat free at our table reserved for you forthwith.'

All three of us sniggered before Beaumont looked at me in confusion what to say back. I spoke for him.

'Sorry Mum, it's an emergency. Beaumont is giving us a lift somewhere.'

'To the hospital,' Noah announced dramatically. I wasn't going to tell her the destination, for reasons that will be apparent in a couple of seconds.

'The hospital? The hospital! Oh my God, what's wrong, Edward, what's wrong? Are you okay, do you need me there? You know I'm always there for you.'

'Mum, mum, no, listen, I'm fine,' I tried to explain over her. 'It's nothing for you to worry about, something I'm helping Appleby with. Listen, though, I need to ask you something. It's really important.'

That got her to listen. 'Yes, of course, anything. What is it?'

I knew it was a strange question, but I had to check my theory. 'Mum, when Alfie came out to you, did you already know? Did you always know he was gay?'

Mum, for once, went quiet. I waited a few moments. 'Mum, did you hear me? Are you there?'

'Hi Edward, yes, she's here. We all heard you, we're all at the table. What's going on?'

I wasn't expecting Alfie himself to answer. 'Sorry, Alfie, I know what I asked must seem weird. But it's for the Kieron Juniper case. I promise it's important, I'll explain later.'

The line went quiet, and I could hear murmured whispers for a few seconds before anyone spoke. 'Hello, Edward, it's Mum again. I don't really understand but I'll answer your question.'

I felt bad at rehashing this for both Mum and Alfie like this. But I needed to prove something. 'Sorry Mum, I only need a yes or no, that's all. Did you always know Alfie was gay?'

'Yes, love, the answer's yes. Yes, I always knew he was gay.'

That was the answer I expected. 'Thank you, Mum. Now Dylan, I hope you don't mind me asking you the same question. Did your mum always know you were gay?'

'For God's sake, Edward!' Alfie shouted. He sounded furious. In all fairness, I was on sensitive ground. Dylan had only come out last year, and it was a tough time for him.

'He's lost the plot,' I heard Dad say.

'I'm sorry, he's not answering that,' Alfie said firmly.

'Yes I am, it's fine,' Dylan spoke up. 'Hi Edward, I'm not sure why you need to know, but I trust you so it must be important.'

'No, you don't need to do this,' I heard Alfie say.

'Edward, you know how difficult it was for Dylan to tell his mum.'

I did. His mum was a strict catholic, and fear of how she might react kept him in the closet until his mid-twenties.

'Yes, it was difficult,' Dylan said. 'But that was because of my hang-ups, not Mum's. She was brilliant. And yes, Edward, she said she always knew deep down. And she didn't care, she said she still loved me the same.'

Again, this was the answer I wanted to get. Even Dylan's mum always knew he was gay, despite it clashing with her strict Catholic views. I said goodbye to my confused and slightly bemused family, promising again to explain later.

'What was all that about?' Beaumont asked from the driver's seat. Having just told me about his own coming out, he must have wondered what on earth I was doing.

'You don't have to worry about the reason for Kieron's murder,' I told him. 'It definitely wasn't because of homophobia.'

'What do you mean, how can you know that?' he asked in confusion.

'Easily. Because Kieron wasn't gay.'

33

I knew something didn't sit right with the things I'd heard in the last couple of days. It was only once Beaumont spoke about his mum's support, I realised what it was: Kieron's mum said she had no clue he was gay, and still didn't believe it.

When Beaumont said his Mum always knew, it made me think. Why didn't Kieron's? That's when I started thinking, what actual evidence did we have that he was gay? What if he wasn't, but it had been made to look like he was?

We had Ellie's outing of him, which had come from Chloe, and Danny. He wasn't in the room to confirm or deny either way.

Then we had his unused coming out statement, which I'd seen on Danny's phone only. We had nothing to prove that Kieron actually wrote it; it could be a fake. I needed to check with Appleby or Wood if the real thing was on Kieron's phone. I suspected it wasn't.

We also had Ellie's confirmation that he admitted it to her, but what did he actually say?

'He just kept saying that it wasn't what I thought, it was much more complex, but we should wait and talk about it at home.' There was nothing there to say he admitted to being gay.

And there was our conversation with Kieron in the toilets when he was really upset. Again, what did he actually say?

'What Ellie said, it ruined everything. But it's not her fault, I can't blame her. She only acted on what Chloe told her. I need to talk to her. Explain what's going on.'

'The biggest dilemma of my life. And I've no idea what I'm supposed to do. Do you stay true to who you are, or go through with a lie for the sake of someone else?'

'I have to be true to myself. Even if it damages someone else. But that's what I'm afraid of.'

None of these comments explicitly confirmed Kieron was gay. But what else could they mean? As I continued to think, I connected to other things from the last two days.

'*Everyone thinks this was because of Kieron coming out, but what if it was because of something he knew that he shouldn't?*'

'*Quite a few of the boys used to come to Kieron with their troubles off the pitch. Danny certainly did. And maybe he knew too much.*'

'*There's a lot you don't know about me: the life I lead and the things I've done. Not everyone would think I'm a very nice person.*'

Most of it made sense now.

Kieron wasn't the gay player hiding in the closet. Danny was.

And it had been the reason for Kieron's murder.

PETER BOON

34

I knew the person I needed to speak to next would be at the hospital, waiting for the man they loved to wake up.

I found who I was looking for sitting in a private family waiting room, the kind that were only available on request and usually impossible to get.

'Hello, Troy.'

To say he looked shocked to see me was an understatement. 'What are you doing here? How the hell did you know I was here?'

'I'm meeting DI Appleby here to help him with something. Because of Danny's suicide attempt.'

I could see his panic as he thought about what to say. 'Oh, I see. I'm here with Chloe, of course, she's just popped out.'

'She hasn't, though, has she? She doesn't know you're here.'

'What, what do you mean?' His voice was high pitched and strained. It was time to put him out of his misery.

'I mean you need to tell the truth. The next person coming to speak to you will be DI Appleby, so why don't you get your story straight with me first?' I gulped. The 'bad cop' act didn't suit me. 'If you tell me the truth, I can help you.'

'The truth?' he said hesitantly, with tears in his eyes.

'That you're in love with Danny. And it's him you've been in a secret relationship with, not Kieron Juniper.'

As soon as I finished speaking, he collapsed into tears. It took ten minutes before he could speak.

And when he did, he finally told me the truth. All of it, his role in everything.

He'd just about got to the end of his story when a nurse knocked on the door of the room.

'Sorry, Troy, you asked me to let you know when there was any news on your friend.'

'Yes?' he said expectantly, jumping up from his seat.

'He's awake, just about, and he's going to be fine.'

'Let's go,' I said as we thanked the nurse and went to follow her out of the room.

I stopped and turned to Troy. 'You know the police will need to speak to you, don't you?'

He nodded, but went to carry on walking. All he seemed to care about now was that Danny was okay.

I cared about that too, but I had another reason for being glad he was alright.

It was time to finally talk to Kieron Juniper's killer.

We knocked on the door and waited to be let in. The response was surprise that the two of us were there, as I expected.

'What are you two doing here?'

I took a deep breath. Perhaps this wasn't very sensitive when Danny had only just woken up, but we had to do it.

'I need to talk to you about Kieron's death. I know that you're the one who cut his brakes.'

'How could you possibly know that?'

'Because we've worked out everything, Chloe.'

DEATH IN THE CLOSET

I'd left Troy to go and see Danny, before going back to Appleby to confirm that Troy had told us what I expected him to. I'd persuaded Appleby to let them have some time together first, but then DC Wood was on hand to arrest him.

We weren't sure how to proceed next, until Appleby's colleague radioed to say that Chloe was leaving the hospital. As soon as I heard that part of the conversation, I slipped off before he had a chance to stop me.

I knew he wouldn't allow me to go with him, so I left the hospital before him and jumped in a taxi. I knew he'd come himself in his unmarked car; he wouldn't want Chloe being alarmed by a police vehicle.

I was probably acting foolishly. I just wanted to be the one to see this through: for Kieron, for Danny, even for Beaumont. However, the one part of my plan that had gone wrong was Noah jumping into the taxi back seat right behind me. It was one thing to put myself in danger, but not Noah.

I'd tried everything to make him go back in the taxi, but he was having none of it. 'We're a detective duo.'

'What do you mean, you've worked out everything?' Chloe said, as she allowed us to follow her in. 'They've arrested Ricky Roberts. They're bound to charge him, they've got overwhelming evidence.'

'And how would you know that, exactly?' I challenged.

'I don't have to put up with this,' she spat. 'My fiancé's in critical condition in hospital.'

'Oh we know, we followed you from there,' Noah said.

I saw her rage building, so I spoke again before she could direct it at Noah. 'Yes, ever the loving fiancée. You stayed just long enough to see he wasn't dead, then left him to see the person who really loves him. Your best friend, Troy Nicholson.'

Her face was a picture of absolute shock. 'You can't know this, you can't, it's not possible.'

'Is that an admission of guilt?' Noah asked cheerfully. I took a couple of steps in front of him. If anything was to happen, I wanted her to attack me, not him. I'd assessed the danger as fairly minimal; cutting brakes was the most cowardly, non-direct murder method possible. But she was still a murderer.

She fumed at Noah's comment as I continued. 'We do know, though. Troy is probably giving his statement to the police as we speak. And Danny will do shortly as soon as he's well enough.'

She paced back and forward a couple of steps, wringing her hands together. 'No, you're bluffing. You know nothing. It's all a load of rubbish, anyway. Kieron was the gay one, not Danny. But that wasn't the reason for his death. Ricky Roberts killed him to cover up his gambling problems.'

'Yes, that's what we were supposed to think,' I said. 'And I will give it to you. That was the last part of the case I couldn't work out. I didn't understand how Ricky Roberts' DNA came to be on the murder weapon. The murder weapon that was, of course, only found the next day, having been dumped in the football club's rubbish for the police to find. How convenient.'

'I've no idea what you're talking about,' she replied, in an attempt to be dismissive.

I continued apace, in hindsight perhaps getting a little too carried away with the melodrama. It later confused me how my nerves even allowed me to confront her like that; I think I was just running on adrenaline.

'And how convenient that you were in a position to blackmail Ricky Roberts' hairdresser. The man who was in a secret relationship with your fiancé, and who cut Ricky's hair the morning after the murder. It must have been easy for Troy to hand you his hairbrush or scissors with Ricky's DNA all over it.'

'How the hell did you...' she stopped herself. 'That's rubbish. Troy doesn't even cut Ricky's hair.'

'He does. I heard he cut most of the team's hair. And Ricky definitely got his hair cut the next morning, he said so on the microphone and I could tell when I saw him.'

'That's all circumstantial, it means nothing,' she sneered.

'Yes, you're right, but what's not circumstantial is Troy's full confession. You can't blackmail him anymore, Chloe. He's willing to be honest about how you forced him to help frame Roberts, and his relationship with Danny, not the fake one with Kieron you made him tell the press. And you can't threaten to ruin him anymore; on reflection, your misdeeds are far worse than his anyway.'

'That little snake betrayed me with my fiancé!' she shouted, showing genuine anger for the first time. 'He deserves everything he gets. But he won't be getting my fiancé. He's mine.'

I had her. 'And there we go, that's the truth of it. The reason Kieron had to die.'

'What the hell are you talking about, you stupid little weasel?'

I looked around the massive open plan house that we stood in. It was tasteless – bright pink everywhere – but it was ridiculously expensive.

'You had no intention of giving up all of this. This house, this lifestyle, all the couple magazine deals. At least not until you had a wedding ring on your finger. I dread to think how much money you'd make on the exclusives for that. Plus half of everything Danny's worth when you filed for divorce afterwards.'

'Rubbish,' she snarled, but she looked panicked.

'That's why you turned a blind eye to Danny's sexuality. Fiona told me the rumours that you both discreetly cheat on each other and carry on, only we thought Danny's flings were with women. What was it Fiona said? *Not quite a relationship of convenience but not far off.*'

''You're going to listen to that head-case? Look at the state of her, she doesn't even know the right decade to dress in.'

I felt my temper rise at this, but I continued calmly. 'But what you weren't counting on was Danny cracking. He had mental health issues anyway, and living a lie was getting too much for him. So he confided in his best friend and Captain, Kieron.'

'No, no, no,' she repeated with quiet fury. I was close to the final truth, and she knew it.

'Kieron advised Danny to tell the truth: to break up with you and come out. He even helped Danny write a coming out statement, which you blackmailed Danny into passing off as Kieron's.

'My theory is, the day of the reception, or perhaps a day or two before, Danny told you everything. About Troy, about Kieron helping him to come out. You couldn't let that happen. Even after the murder, you thought of everything. You visited Ellie and manipulated her into suspecting Ricky Roberts. You even tried to do it to us, too.'

She laughed out loud this time. 'Go on. What happened next? This would make a fantastic story. You should get in touch with ITV and offer to help them reboot *Footballers' Wives*. But this doesn't happen in real life, hun.'

'It's very over-dramatic, I admit. But that's why you nearly got away with it. And it's funny you mention that TV show, because you'd have done anything to become a footballer's wife. Including lying to Ellie that it was Kieron who was gay, coaxing her into making a public scene, then cutting the brakes of Kieron's car before he got the chance to tell her the truth.'

'That's ridiculous. Kieron *had a* chance to tell Ellie the truth. You claim to know everything, so you must know that she spoke to him, before she went on the microphone. Why didn't he tell her then? In fact, why wouldn't he walk into that room and tell everyone he wasn't the gay one?'

'Ooh, I know the answer to this one!' Noah said, waving his hand in the air. 'To protect Danny.'

'That's right,' I agreed. 'To protect Danny's mental health. He would have known what a delicate way his friend was in, and if he'd outed Danny – the only way to explain the truth to Ellie – he could have sent him into a terrible state, like the one he's only just survived today. Kieron even said to me it was the biggest dilemma of his life. But he would have told the truth soon, which you couldn't risk. The last thing he said to me was he had to tell the truth, *even if it damages someone else.* He would have persuaded Danny to come out, your time was nearly up.'

'Have you quite finished? Because I'm bored with this now. Time for you two weirdos to go.'

I stood my ground. 'No. You need to admit the truth.'

She cackled hideously. 'Even if I do, who's going to believe you two? And you think I can't get Troy to withdraw his statement? He'll do anything I tell him to.'

'You're sure about that, are you?' I said. I felt my heart racing, sensing danger for the first time. I'd estimated that Appleby would have been here by now.

'Be careful, boys. I sent Kieron to his death without him even knowing. Who knows what I could do to you two, when you're least expecting it.'

'Then you're admitting it?' Noah said, but I couldn't tell if he meant it as a question or a statement.

'So what if I am? Like I said, I've got Troy in my pocket and I'm not worried about you two. Otherwise, there's no proof.'

'Except this,' Noah said, taking his phone out of his pocket and cheerfully showing us it was on voice recording mode. 'Sorry, I forgot to tell you this time.'

'You little freak!' she screamed. 'Give that to me.' She flung herself towards him and knocked him to the floor, grabbing for the phone as she writhed above him.

I froze in terror for a second before I realised I had to save him. I reached to grab her when the door opened. It must have been Appleby, finally.

It wasn't.

'Get off my friend, you evil bitch!' Fiona yelled as she rugby tackled Chloe off Noah, sending her flying to the ground and landing on top of her. Chloe struggled below her, but Fiona wasn't having it. She was much stronger than I thought, even holding her down with one hand while getting her phone out. 'Smile for the camera, Chloe!'

'Don't even think about printing that,' Chloe spat venomously.

'Oh I won't,' Fiona said with a grin. 'This is just for my personal enjoyment. To remember you by.'

Finally, DI Appleby and DC Wood ran in with a uniformed officer, who ran straight to Chloe with handcuffs.

'Can I say it?' I heard Wood ask Appleby. 'It's my first murder arrest.'

'Fine,' nodded Appleby, looking bemused.

'Chloe Stone, you are under arrest on suspicion of the murder of Kieron Juniper. You do not have to say anything, but it may harm your defence if you do not mention when questioned something you later rely on in court. Anything you do say may be given in evidence.'

'Get off me, get off me, don't you know who I am?' Chloe shrieked as the PC took her away. 'I'll have your careers for this!'

'Edward, you're a bloody idiot for going off by yourself, you could have got killed!' Appleby said furiously as we checked on Noah.

'Lucky I was there to save them,' Fiona quipped, winking at me.

'How did you even know we were here?' I asked.

'Remember, I told Noah not to go off investigating without me,' she said. 'I don't have a tracking device, but I managed to enable 'find my phone' on his mobile when he wasn't looking.'

'Nice one!' Noah said, either not realising or not caring that she'd invaded his privacy. 'Another case solved and a great story to write. I think the three of us make a great team.'

'I do too,' Fiona said, winking at me.

36

'Are you sure this is the right thing to do?' Beaumont asked as we stood outside the closed door.

'Definitely,' I replied. It was the next day, and I'd come back to the hospital. There was something I needed to do, and it involved Beaumont. I knocked gently on the door to the private room before entering.

'Edward,' Danny said as soon as he saw me, trying to sit himself up in panic. 'I'm sorry, I'm so sorry. I didn't know she was the murderer. She convinced me it was Roberts.'

'Relax, Danny, it's fine,' I tried to tell him. 'She manipulated everyone.'

'It's not fine,' he said. 'I played my part in Kieron's death, and I'll have to live with that for the rest of my life.'

'Which I hope is a very long time,' I said. 'You've got a lot to live for, Danny.'

He smiled, but then looked confused as Beaumont stepped into the room. 'Beaumont? Hello mate, what are you doing here?'

'Hi there. How are you feeling?' Beaumont asked with a shy smile.

'I've brought Beaumont along because you two have a lot in common. I think it will do you good to have a chat.'

Danny still looked confused as Beaumont took a seat next to the bed.

'Beaumont has something to tell you,' I said as I moved back towards the door.

Beaumont looked at me and nodded before turning back to Danny. 'I'm gay. And I believe I'm not the only one.'

I watched as Danny's shock turned into relief and then happiness. He burst out laughing, and Beaumont soon joined him.

'No gay Premier League players ever and now there's two in one team, what are the chances?' Beaumont said.

'Roberts will definitely quit now,' Danny said before they laughed again.

'I'll leave you to it,' I said, as I made my way out of the room.

'Edward?' I stopped at the sound of Danny's voice. 'Thank you. Thank you for everything. I don't know what I'm going to do, but I'll spend every day making this up to Kieron. Being the man he knew I could be.'

'And I'll help you. We can take this journey together,' Beaumont said, putting his fist out to bump Danny's.

I stepped out of the room to see Fiona waiting on the other side of the door.

'What are you doing here?' we both said at the same time.

She spoke first. 'You caught me. I was going to see if Danny was ready to talk. There's a lot of bad press out there on him already with his part in Kieron's death. I thought I could get his side, you know, maybe finally get my story. Now Chloe's stopped leaking all the stories she wanted out.'

'I don't think he's ready for it,' I said. 'He's got a lot to think about before he speaks to anyone.'

'I understand,' she said. 'I shouldn't have come, really. All of this has made me realise that people's lives are more important than what's in the press.'

'Oh no, don't give up,' I said. 'Danny might not be ready to talk to you, but I know someone else who is. How would you like a world exclusive, history making interview?'

'I'd love that. Who is it?' she replied with excitement.

'I'll tell you in a minute, there's one condition first.'

'What is it?' she asked, looking confused.

I breathed in and out slowly. This was it. I took her hand. 'The condition is, will you go for a drink with me?'

I watched comprehension arrive on her face. 'Like a date?'

I nodded. 'Like a date.'

'Edward, I'd love to.'

BEAUMONT ALBRIGHT WORLD EXCLUSIVE: "I'M A GAY FOOTBALLER"

By Fiona Turtle

Beachy Head United's newest signing has made history by being the first Premier League footballer ever to publicly confirm that he is gay.

Beaumont, 18, has been openly gay to his family and close friends since he was 16, and describes it as 'no big deal.'

We can reveal that he has come out to his entire team on a social media group chat, and has been overwhelmed by the support he has received from his teammates.

Beaumont wants to be an inspiration as the first openly gay role model in English Premiership football and hopes that fans will embrace the news: *'I'm a footballer first, but this is part of who I am, along with my race, and I hope that supporters and football fans will accept me for who I am.'*

Beaumont has the full support of his club. Jackie Luton, Beaumont's agent, said: *'I've spoken to the board at Beachy Head United, and they confirmed how proud they are of Beaumont. They want to pass on that he is a brave, brilliant young man and they are looking forward to his future with the club.'*

Beaumont himself added: *'I want to thank my mum, family, friends and teammates for all the support I've received so far.*

'I want to dedicate this moment to two men who have really inspired me. Kieron Juniper: a great man and a great role model who I only wish I got to know more. He loved his club, his parents and his fiancée, Ellie, very much and none of us will be the same without him. I'm dedicating my first game this weekend to him.'

'And Danny Higgins, a man who has really supported me in these last few days. He has made mistakes and he will share them with you in time. But please give him space until that time, and on his behalf, please don't believe everything you read in the meantime.'

The team here at Chalk Gap Observer would like to send our very best wishes to Beaumont and give him our full support.

Comments

What a legend *claps*

I'm not crying, you're crying.

Now that's how you do it. Classy guy. Lovely tribute to Juniper too.

History made in our own little village. Get in Beaumont.

I'm reading this story all the way in the USA and I just want to say congratulations, my man. Way to go.

That's right Beaumont, you do you! A lesson for us all.

Hope Higgins follows suit and doesn't retire. They can help each other, you've got this boys.

And only 18 too. Inspirational.

'No big deal,' how it should be. Hope anyone else who needs to comes forward.

For all who came before him, who retired first or didn't come out at all. He represents you too. You're all brave in your own ways. Respect always.

Get the next in the Edward Crisp series, the novella *Death In A Deckchair,* now:

https://www.amazon.co.uk/dp/B0BC4ZYMQZ

And get a FREE ebook novella, *The Mystery Of Jackson King,* when you join my mailing list here:

https://bookhip.com/NXRFHV

The Edward Crisp Mysteries:

Who Killed Miss Finch

The Snow Day Murders

The Mystery of Jackson King (novella)

Death In The Closet

Death In A Deckchair (novella)

Ten Green Bottles (Out November 22)

Author's Note

Before I get to my usual acknowledgments, I just want to say a little about this book, as it's by far the most personal one so far.

I've had the idea of writing about a gay footballer coming out for a long time; years ago I even started the project as a gay rom com! The fact that there is an entire multi-billion pound industry with hardly any gay men, certainly not in top flight English football anyway, has interested me for a long time.

For the men who have come out (as mentioned in Noah's research), the last social media post on Beaumont's article, and therefore the last words of the novel, was actually me sneaking my own comment in there! Robbie, Thomas, Thomas, Liam, Justin (RIP), anyone else I may have missed, those openly gay in another sport, or those yet to make that step or choosing not to, you have my respect and love always.

I'd also like to add a note about the player coming out being 25; this was the age that I came out (long story, I'll save it for the autobiography!) so I deliberately chose that age, and was able to bring some of my own experiences into that.

Luckily, in the 17 years since coming out I have been very lucky to have not really received any hatred or abuse, which I know isn't true for the whole LGBT community; as I tried to show in some of the social media comments I added in this novel, we do have some work to do.

You will also notice I gave this book's dedication to my family. They were all so fantastic at the time (and have continued to be) and made the most difficult step to take as easy as possible. Thank you all for your love and support.

Also a thank you to the friends who helped me through that journey at the time. You know who you are.

Usual book-related thank yous on the next page, I just wanted to take the rare opportunity to thank the people who were a part of that time of my life. This book is for all of you!

Acknowledgments

My third novel! (And fourth book: thank you to everyone for accepting my novella *The Mystery of Jackson King* into your hearts as part of the Edward Crisp canon, it was totally unexpected, you treated it like it was a proper novel!)

The last ten months as a published author have been more than I could ever have hoped for. I still pinch myself that my little mysteries have found themselves such lovely readers, and it has been an absolute pleasure interacting with lots of you on social media, as well as reading your kind reviews. Thank you to every single one of you who's left a review, sent me a message, said kind words or recommended my books to someone. A special mention to Susan Wilson and Maggie Hall (my dear childhood teacher) who very kindly share pretty much everything I post!

As mentioned on the previous page, this is one that's very personal to me and I loved writing it. I hope you enjoyed it and found the balance right between the usual fun stuff and the more serious subject matter. I'd also be interested to know readers' thoughts on the couple of different things I tried this time: the notes from the footballer, the newspaper articles, and the social media comments accompanying them. Would you like to see these kinds of things in future novels? Let me know on social media or at peter@peterboonauthor.com.

This one wouldn't have been what it was without my fantastic team.

Thanks as ever to Marion and Ben, the fantastic husband and wife team who are my first port of call for most things.

Next to my friend Charlie, who surpassed himself this time with some fantastic character names. You're so much better at it than me (even if I didn't go with Beachy Head Harriers in the end). Thank you, mate!

Then, to my incredible proof reading team: Sue (Mum), Kerry, Hannah, Michelle, Lisa, Charlotte, Zoe, Lesley, Phillip, Donna and Sam. You are all amazing and I love chatting about my books with you (and getting your reactions in real time!).

I also want to give a massive thank you to Samantha Brownley and all the admins and readers at UK Crime Book Club who have given me such fantastic support, and Donna Morfett at Donna's Interviews Reviews and Giveaways. These two Facebook groups are such an amazing help to authors in finding readers, particularly newer or indie authors, and Sam, Donna et al have been amazing. I loved my interviews with both of you.

I've mentioned my family already on the previous page, but thank you as ever for your love and support. And massive thanks to all my friends, old and new, north and south, for your friendship.

Finally, Graeme, there aren't enough words to thank you for all you do for me. Love always.

PETER BOON